THE FARM MYSTERY SERIES:

THE
MYSTERIOUS
MESSAGE

By Mr. and Mrs. Stephen B. Castleberry

Castleberry Farms Press

Cover art © was created by: Jeffrey T. Larson, 11947 E. State Rd. 13, Maple, Wisconsin 54854 (715) 364-8473

All scripture references are from the King James Version of the Bible.

Castleberry Farms Press
P.O. Box 337
Poplar, WI 54864

Printed in the U.S.A.

ISBN 1-891907-04-2

e-mail: cbfarmpr@pressenter.com

Visit us at: www.pressenter.com/~cbfarmpr

A Note From the Authors

In *The Mysterious Message*, the second book in *The Farm Mystery Series*, you will learn of a special ministry called the Voice of the Martyrs. This ministry provides Bibles, food, clothing, and other help to Christians around the world who are persecuted for their faith. A prayer calendar, books, free homeschool study materials (called LINK International), and further information are available from: Voice of the Martyrs, P.O. Box 443, Bartlesville, OK 74005, (800) 747-0085, email address is vomusa@aol.com.

Our primary goal in publishing is to provide wholesome books in a manner that brings honor to our Lord Jesus Christ. We always welcome your comments, suggestions, and most importantly, your prayers.

In the back of this book is information about the other titles we have published. If you would like to contact us, you can reach us at this address:

Mr. and Mrs. Stephen B. Castleberry
Castleberry Farms Press
P.O. Box 337
Poplar, WI 54864

Chapter One

Jason! Do you think it's wise for you to do that?" Andy looked wide-eyed as his twelve-year-old brother boldly put his hands on the cover of the bee hive. "I mean, what if thousands of bees come flying out and start stinging you?"

Jason tried to look brave, yet he too felt apprehensive. Looking at ten-year-old Andy, he tried to decide what he should do. Finally he replied, "I'm not worried about it, Andy. I've done this before, you know."

"Sure, but Cathy or Dad were always with you," Andy cautioned.

That was a fact of which Jason was aware. In fact, if the truth be told, he had been thinking about that very fact before Andy mentioned it. Jason tried to think clearly. "Cathy said she needed the mystery solved. If she thought it was somehow unsafe for us to look at the bees, don't you think she would have said something about it? Besides, we told Mom we were going to look at the hives, and she said it was okay."

"I know she did. But you're a lot braver than I am!" Andy took a few steps back to watch Jason from a safer distance.

All bee hives have a top cover. In fact, most have two covers. The outer cover is designed to be a barrier from wind and rain, and is usually held on with a concrete block or other heavy object. Jason had already tossed off the rock holding the outer cover of this hive.

Jason thought, *I've either got to do it now or just walk away.* It would be an understatement to say that his nerves were a bit on edge.

Carefully, slowly, Jason lifted off the outer cover of the bee hive. His courage rebounded as no bees came flying out. "See, it's going to be okay," he said, smiling at Andy. Next, he tried to remove the inner cover, but it was stuck on pretty well. The bees had sealed it with propolis, a sticky, gummy substance that bees use to block holes and seal along cracks. Amazingly, bees collect this glue from tree sap, just as God taught them to do.

Even though it was the first week in December and about 55 degrees, Jason started to sweat. With his tool, he pried around all sides of the inside cover. There, it was almost loose. "Now if I can just get this one corner off . . ."

Jason found the strength he needed to pry the last corner loose. In fact, he had so much strength that the inside cover of the bee hive went sailing into the air and crashed on the ground a few feet away.

At first only a few bees came out to investigate the damage and the "damager." Jason and Andy didn't pay much attention to them. "It looks like there are plenty of bees to me," Jason stated. "I wonder why Cathy thought we were losing bees?" Jason was a little surprised at his own level of calm while looking down at thousands of bees. Andy, too, was feeling pretty grown up about the whole situation.

Now, bees can be quiet and peaceful little creatures. However, anyone can get a bit perturbed when

The Mysterious Message

you start jolting their house and tearing off their roof. Alarm among the bees began to spread, and before long the air was filled with buzzing, irritated bees. The boys were so intent on thinking about their mystery that they didn't notice the increase in "air traffic" for a few moments. By the time they did, it was too late.

"Hey . . . uh-oh, there's a bunch of bees . . . Jason, there's a bee on your face . . . ouch! . . . we'd better run!" Andy cried, taking his own advice and running away from the hive while trying to wave the bees from his face. This just stirred the bees to higher indignation. First one bee, then another, left its poisonous stinger in Andy's skin. "Ouch!" he cried out as he ran. "Mom! Cathy! Somebody get them off me! Ouch!"

Jason had troubles of his own. He was quickly trying to replace the inner cover and top on the hive, which was especially dangerous as bees were landing all over them. He got stung several times doing this, then was stung a few more times as he raced away.

By the time they reached the house, the boys were very unhappy and in a great deal of pain. As Mom administered some healing ointment on the stings, the boys unsuccessfully fought back tears.

"Oh boys!" Mom exclaimed as she continued to remove stingers and doctor the boys. "Whatever did you get into?"

"It was one of our bee hives, Mom," Jason said between sobs. "We took the cover off to look inside." He couldn't continue because of the pain. Andy, too, was in no shape to answer questions at this time.

"I know I said you could look at the hives. But I

didn't know you would take the cover off!" Mom exclaimed, wiping away Jason's tears. "God must have used the bees this morning, to teach you a lesson about wisdom and caution. But we can talk about that later. Why don't you guys go sit on the back porch a minute? Maybe the cooler air will help take your mind off these stings. I'll prepare a herbal tea for you that will help take away your pain."

Although the pain was terrible, it was good to have Mom taking care of them. It was easy to see Mom's love by the way she moved so quickly and the concern in her expression. She was well known in their Tennessee town as one who had great compassion. Everyone was thankful to see Connie Nelson's appearance when something bad happened. Of course, the same could be said for their father, Timothy Nelson, as well. The boys were blessed to have Mom and Dad as examples in demonstrating Christian love and kindness.

Both boys got up and walked to the porch. It wasn't easy. Their legs and arms were starting to swell here and there from the bee venom. After sipping on Mom's herbal tea a few minutes, the boys began talking about their mystery. The pain, however, persisted.

Chapter Two

It had begun innocently enough that Monday morning. Andy and his six-year-old brother, Ben, were in the basement washing out some barn buckets. Because Ben had poured in a little too much soap, there were many bubbles. Grabbing a paper airplane, Andy decided to put some bubbles on an airplane and see what would happen when the plane was flown across the room. It was a huge success, with bubbles dropping like bombs as the plane flew. So, the boys did it again and again. Jason walked in and watched the planes with interest.

Cathy, the boys' sister, was washing clothes in the basement. "Say guys, I have a mystery that maybe you can help me with," she began. Jason and Andy operated a small detective agency, called The Great Detective Agency, out of their basement. They had solved a number of mysteries and were always looking for new cases. Being more interested in solving a case than becoming millionaires, they never charged for their services. Mom and Dad had often provided them with mysteries, but this was the first time that Cathy had elicited their help.

"This one is not a real big deal, at least not yet," Cathy continued. "It seems to me that we are beginning to lose some bees. I checked on them a few days ago and their numbers just seemed to be less. Think you can help me figure it out?"

"Sure!" both boys chimed in together. This was just the kind of mystery that they liked to solve. It would be possible to gather all the clues they needed, since the bee hives were on their property and they didn't have to cross the road to get to them. Also, they would be helping their family if they could solve the problem. Jason grabbed the small, spiral notebook that he always kept in his back pocket for such situations. "What can you tell us about their disappearance? When did you first notice it?"

Cathy smiled at his determination and enthusiasm. "I guess I first noticed it about three weeks ago. Like I said, it's not a big deal yet. I may just be imagining it. But if we are losing bees, I would like to get to the bottom of it before it's too late." Fifteen-year-old Cathy was the beekeeper in the Nelson household and was responsible for their care. It was a job she thoroughly enjoyed.

"Could it be a swarm, Cathy?" Andy asked with a pencil poised near his own notebook.

"I don't think so," Cathy replied. "Bees swarm in the summer. While we have had some unusually warm weather lately, I think it would be highly unlikely they would swarm. Besides, if that were the case, I would think I would have nothing left but an empty beehive."

"True," Jason said thoughtfully, trying to think of other explanations. "Didn't you mention one time something about disease? Do bees get diseases and die? Maybe that's it." Jason was hoping secretly that such a simple explanation wouldn't be sufficient. He was looking forward to solving what he hoped was a hard-to-solve mystery.

Cathy threw some more towels into the dryer and

cleaned the filter. "Yes, bees do get diseases. I suppose that's a possibility, Jason. It would be reasonable that not all the bees would die at once. I would notice some more missing each time I looked. Yes, that's a possibility."

Jason was pleased that he had suggested a viable solution. "We'll check into that!" he said. "Can you think of any other possibilities?"

Before she could answer, Ben offered a solution. He had been listening to this conversation, hoping to add something of value. "I think I know what it is," he said. "I think they're getting lost! Maybe they're flying out of their house looking for flowers, and then when they turn around, they can't remember the way back!"

"I suppose that could happen, Ben, except that there are no flowers this time of year. They aren't flying out to find them."

Ben didn't seem the least bit fazed by this rejection of his idea. Instead he offered up another possible solution. "Maybe they're getting blown right out of their house! You know it's been windy today!"

"We'll check into that," Jason said. "I'm not sure about it, but we'll sure check that out, Ben."

Later that morning, when the boys had permission from Mom, they decided to go and investigate the hives. It had seemed a perfectly harmless thing to do. The weather had been warm lately, but today it was cool enough that the bees shouldn't be flying too much. They had walked to the three sets of hives and studied them carefully. Each hive now seemed short and squatty with only two boxes on each. Depending on the summer and if the honey was "flowing" well, sometimes the hives had six layers. But by this time of year, the honey from the top layers had been removed by Cathy and was now safely in jars in the cupboard.

"How would we tell if they had some disease?" Andy asked.

"I guess we would see sick or dead bees," Jason replied. They looked around on the ground around the hives but didn't see many dead bees. "Bees really take care of their hives and keep them clean," Jason informed Andy. "If they had dead bees in there, they would drag them to the outside and drop them out of the hive. It doesn't look like there are many here, though. At least not so many that Cathy would notice the hive population getting smaller."

Andy crawled around the hives looking closely. This was something that he would definitely not try during the middle of summer, when thousands of bees were busily flying in and out of the hives. But today, there were only a few leaving the hives and returning. "Say, Jason. Isn't it possible that a bunch of bees are dead inside the hives, but the others are too sick to drag the dead ones out? Maybe there aren't many out here because they are still inside the hive. What do you think?"

Excitedly, Jason jumped to his feet. "Maybe you're onto something, Andy. Let's take a look!" Having said that, Jason walked to a nearby tree and grabbed a small red pry bar designed specifically for helping separate bee hives. Cathy kept the pry bar hanging from a nail on the tree so it would always be there when she wanted to work with her bees.

"What are you going to do?" Andy had asked.

"I'm going to take the top off and look down into

this hive," Jason had replied confidently.

The rest of the story was still painfully in their minds (and their bodies). As they were recapping the morning's events, Cathy came out on the porch. "Are you guys all right? Mom said you got stung!" Then when she got close enough to see the swelling that had already taken place, she got down and looked into the boys' faces. "Oh boys," she said sadly. "You really got stung badly! I'm so sorry! I would never have asked you to get involved in my problem if I thought it would come to this." Cathy was really worried about them.

"Mom said we're going to be okay," Andy replied weakly. "Don't worry about it, Cathy. It was our fault. We were trying to look inside the hive when we got stung."

"Yes, that probably wasn't a good idea," Jason admitted sheepishly. "I'm the one who suggested it. I should have known better." After shifting himself to a more comfortable position, he added, "I hope we didn't hurt your bees any, Cathy."

"Did you put the top back on?" she asked quickly, a look of new concern in her eyes.

"Yes, it's all put back together," Jason said, remembering vividly the pain that simple act had caused him. Then, getting back to the case, he asked her, "If it was some kind of a disease, would the bees drag off the dead ones right away, or would they wait to do it?"

Cathy wasn't sure where this was leading, but answered, "I don't really know. I suppose they would remove the dead ones as soon as possible. Bees are very clean animals and like to keep their house neat and tidy." Then she added, "Did you notice very many bees when you lifted off the top? Is it my imagination, or are there fewer bees in the hives?"

Jason and Andy looked at each other, with pain showing in their expressions. Andy spoke for the pair. "Judging by how I feel right now, I would say there are plenty!" Then addressing Mom, who had come out to get the tea cups, he asked, "Is there something else we can do, Mom? The stings still hurt. A lot!"

"I'm afraid not," Mom said in a soothing voice. "Maybe you two would like to come inside and have me read to you?"

Slowly both boys rose and walked into the living room. As Mom was choosing a book, Jason looked over at Andy, who seemed to be in as much misery as himself. "This is one case that we're going to have to go a little bit slower on, partner."

"You can sure say that again!" Andy agreed. Before they could begin discussing the case anymore, Mom sat down and began reading. This was fine with the boys. They were happy to have a diversion from bees (and stings) for a while!

Later that evening, the boys felt like discussing the Case of the Missing Bees again. "What are we going to do now?" asked Andy.

"I've been thinking about it most of the day," Jason answered. "It seems to me that we forgot to check one of the most obvious possibilities. It could be a predator. Maybe some animal is trying to get at the honey, and in doing so is killing some of the bees. Or maybe, the bees are attacking something that is trying to steal their honey and they are sort of clinging to that animal as the animal runs away. That would sure explain it."

"Yes, I guess it could. Well, looks like we need to look for some tracks," Andy agreed.

Dad heard the tail-end of this conversation. "Whatever tracks you are going to look at will have to wait until tomorrow. It's time for our family devotions right now. Have you seen Ben anywhere?"

"I think he's still up in our bedroom, Dad," Jason answered. "The last time I saw him, he was sitting on his bed, gluing some old stamps on a sheet of paper."

"Gluing? Did you say gluing . . ." Dad quickly left the room, muttering something about ruining the blanket with the glue. In a few minutes he returned and the family prepared for their nightly time of Bible reading.

After reading about God's provision for Israel through Joshua, Dad reached for the Voice of the Martyr's prayer calendar from the desk beside his chair. "Tonight we want to remember to pray for the boys in Sudan who are forced to learn the Koran. We need to pray that they would hunger and thirst for the Word of God," he read from the calendar. Almost as soon as he finished saying this, Ben's hand was waving in the air. "What is it, Ben?" asked Dad.

"Who's the Koran, and why are we praying for him?"

Dad patiently explained that the Koran was the holy book for Moslems. He went on to explain that in the African country of Sudan, boys are forced to study and memorize the Koran, even if they are Christians.

"That's not nice!" Ben decided quickly. "They

shouldn't do that."

"You're right," Dad agreed seriously. "Remember that there are people all over the world who are persecuting Christians and making them do things they don't want to do." Looking at his family, he continued, "It's very sad. That's why we pray for them daily. These are our brothers and sisters in Christ, and they are suffering just because they are Christians. Of course, some are suffering in even worse ways, enduring all manner of arrest, prison, torture, and even giving their lives because they are Christians. I'm reminded of the verse in Hebrews 13 which commands us to remember the Christians who are in prison just as though we were also in prison. We are also to remember those who suffer just as if our bodies also suffered for Christ."

"It sure is more fun to live in Tennessee," Ben said gravely.

"I have to admit it is much easier to live here in Tennessee, son. God has blessed us. We never know when that blessing may be removed, though. Also, we need to remember those who are living where it isn't 'so much fun' — that God would give them strength, endurance, and determination to live for Christ. They have to rely on the Holy Spirit, just like we do. Let's pray for them now."

As he finished speaking, the Nelson family got on their knees and prayed for the persecuted church. Ben's prayer expressed in simple terms what each was praying: "God, thank You that we live where we can have fun. Please help those who are living where they don't have fun because they're Christians. I don't want to forget them. I'm glad You won't forget them.

The Mysterious Message

In Jesus' name, Amen."

It was painful for Andy to rise to his feet. Several stings on his legs had caused swelling and the pain had never fully gone away. *Still*, he thought, *I'm blessed. What are a few bee stings compared to what boys my age must be going through in other countries right now. Tonight! God, help me not to complain*, he prayed silently.

As he drifted off to sleep, Andy thought of all the things he had that were a blessing from God. He lived in a country where he could read and study the Bible without fear of being arrested. The police weren't going to arrest his father and put his father in jail for teaching his family about God. People weren't going to burn his house or steal his things just because he was a Christian. Yes, Andy and his family had many things for which to be thankful.

Chapter Three

On the next morning, Tuesday, Andy woke up feeling sore all over. "Hey, Jason, are you as sore as I am?" he asked.

Before Jason could answer, Ben replied, "I'm sure sore. Sore all over. I think I must have had a dream where I walked a long way or something! Jason, are you sore?" he echoed Andy's question. Ben so wanted to be one of the big boys.

Jason began to grin, but then a painful look covered his face. "Ow. Just smiling hurts." Jason had a bee sting in a particularly painful location, his left cheek. "I'll tell you one thing. I'm sure not going to mess with the bees today!"

"But don't we need to solve the mystery?" Andy asked. "After all, you know our motto: When we START a case, We FINISH a case!"

Jason tried to bring logic to the situation. "Yes, of course. We'll finish the case. But our motto doesn't say **when** we will finish it." He laughed, but then quickly his expression changed to pain again, the penalty for using the facial muscles so soon after a bee sting.

"I think I might know what the problem is," Ben spoke up, as he finished buttoning his shirt. "Someone is coming in during the night and stealing our bees."

At first Andy was going to laugh at this comment. However, the more he thought about it, the more plausible it seemed. Why couldn't that be what was happening? It seemed like people were willing to steal anything these days. He even remembered Dad telling about someone who stole a huge garbage dumpster, the kind they have to haul away with a big truck. And it was loaded with garbage at the time!

"What do you think, Jason? Maybe someone is stealing our bees?"

"I doubt it, although I suppose anything is possible," Jason commented. "It wouldn't do them any good. Bees aren't going to work unless there is a queen bee present, as far as I understand. I think bees live together, like in a colony, and everyone works together for the good of the colony. So, even if someone stole, say a thousand bees, he probably couldn't get them to make any honey."

That logic made sense to Andy. But Ben wasn't convinced. "What if the stealer didn't want to make honey with the bees? What if he just wanted to get the bees to use them for something else?"

"Like what?" asked Jason.

"Well, maybe he is going to use them to sting people with," Ben replied seriously.

"Our bees would be good for that, if yesterday is any indication!" Jason laughed. Then he screwed up his face again. "I'm going to have to remember not to laugh today. That's really painful. Let's go see if breakfast is ready."

As they walked down the hall, Andy had another thought. "You know, someone could use the stolen bees, even if they didn't get the queen. You can buy a new queen. I remember that Cathy did that last year for our bees."

Jason nodded in agreement. "That's right. We'll have to check into that. But it seems like you would have to steal all the bees at one time for it to work."

The boys reached the kitchen and found Mom busily finishing up preparations for breakfast. The aroma of scrambled eggs and fresh biscuits filled the air. No one had to ask the boys to come and sit down to eat. They planted themselves in their chairs long before it was time to indulge in these treats.

After Dad asked the blessing, everyone began passing food and talking happily. "Boys, I don't want you to take the cover off the hives today," Dad instructed as he scooped some scrambled eggs onto his plate.

"Yes sir. You don't have to worry about that," Jason said, trying to keep his facial muscles from being stretched in any direction. "It's safe to say that I won't do that again for a long time."

"But Dad," Andy began, "can we use the bee smoker, hat, and veils? We'll be careful, and Jason knows how to use the smoker."

"No, I don't want you using the smoker," Dad answered. "Especially since I won't be home. You'd be surprised how fast something can get out of hand."

Jason and Andy both had a pretty good idea about how fast things get out of hand. Yesterday was fresh on their minds.

"Well, how about the hats and the veils?" Andy asked.

"And the overalls and special thick gloves?" Jason added.

Dad looked doubtful. "I don't know. We don't want to ruin those things. They were expensive to buy. Also, they're very important to us during the summer." Then turning his head, he addressed his daughter. "Cathy, are you going to help them today?"

Cathy took another biscuit from the plate as she answered. "Would you like me to, Dad? I had planned on working most of the day on my sewing and some math problems I have been having trouble with, but I could help the boys if you prefer that."

"No, that's okay," Dad said. He looked at the boys. "What are you planning on doing at the hives today?"

"We haven't talked about it yet," Jason replied. "But I know we would like to look over the area a little more carefully. You know, see if there are any tracks or anything like that. Honest, we won't even touch the hives, Dad."

"Okay, I guess I will trust you guys to be careful with our bee supplies. Try not to rip them, though," Dad said.

Mom quickly added, "And don't forget to put things back where you found them."

"Yes ma'am. Yes sir. We'll be careful!" The boys were excited.

Chapter Four

After breakfast, the boys did their chores and then worked on their lessons. Jason spent a good bit of time converting decimals to fractions and fractions to decimals. When he finished, he started working on an essay about beavers. At the top of his paper, he wrote "Beavers . . . by Jason Nelson." Not really wanting to get started, he glanced absently out the window. Then, leaning back lazily in his chair, he said, "Say Andy, do you know anything about beavers?"

Andy had been trying his best to add a column of fractions when this question came. He was happy for the diversion. "Well, not much. I know they live in ponds and make dams. They like to eat wood, too." Then he smiled and added, "I would guess, since they are always gnawing on wood, that they have to go to the dentist a lot more often than we do!"

Jason laughed. But only for a second. "Hey," he reminded Andy, "don't forget that it hurts when I laugh."

"Sorry," Andy said, still giggling under his breath.

"What are you boys doing in there?" Mom asked from the kitchen. "Don't get sidetracked."

"Yes ma'am," both boys answered.

In about thirty minutes, Mom checked their math and helped Jason with ideas on his composition. Finally, she announced, "Okay, why don't you boys go out and get some fresh air now. You can work on this a little more this afternoon."

The boys didn't need a second invitation. "Thanks," they said happily as they raced out of the room.

In the basement, the boys found the bee supplies and started dividing them. "Here, Andy, you can use this bee suit. I think it's the smaller of the two."

Andy put it on and was trying to zip it up when Jason suddenly started laughing, then groaning. "Say, I asked you not to make me laugh," he pleaded.

"I didn't do anything!" Andy replied. Then he started laughing when he saw what Jason looked like in Dad's size large bee suit. "That suit is a little big on you."

"Go look at yourself in the mirror and you'll see why I started laughing," Jason said.

Andy did, and got tickled again. With hats and veils, they looked even funnier. But the gloves were the true finale.

"I wonder if I look like a man who suddenly shrunk in half," Andy said. "I know you do!"

Eventually the boys finished getting "suited up" and headed to the bee hives. They hadn't really expected to have any trouble with the bees today, but after yesterday they weren't willing to take even a slight chance on getting stung. While the suits and other paraphernalia did reduce their fears, they didn't do much in the way of helping them be able to move around easily.

"Are you having as much trouble seeing things as I am?" asked Andy. "Every time I turn my head, this hat tilts and tries to fall off. I find myself keeping my head straight and turning my body to look at something."

Jason nodded. "I'm having a hard enough time just keeping the gloves from falling off my hands."

When they reached the hives, the boys began to examine the area closely. They didn't see any tracks in the grass. At least they didn't see any suspicious tracks. Of course the grass was all crushed where they had stood and walked around yesterday. They looked in a wide circle around the hives trying to see if they could find any tracks. After a few minutes, Jason said, "I guess we aren't going to find anything. Are you ready to head back to the house?"

"Yes," Andy said. "Wearing this stuff isn't as much fun as I thought it would be."

When they were far away from the hives, they took their hats and gloves off. They reached the driveway at about the same time a car was pulling in. Both boys moved to the grass to be safe.

"It's Mr. Johnson. I wonder what he's here for," mused Andy.

"Hi there!" Mr. Johnson said. "I came to borrow your dad's air compressor. You look busy today. Been working with your bees?"

The boys explained their mystery and asked if Mr. Johnson had any ideas. He also kept bees and had done so for many years.

"Well, now let's see," he began. "Given the time of year we are in, I would be surprised if it was disease." He thought some more, then said simply, "Could be ants."

"Ants? Do they like honey?" Jason asked.

"Sure do. They like bees, too. I've read of entire colonies of bees being wiped out by a swarm of ants.

The Mysterious Message

They take the honey. But they also take the bees."

"Wow!" Andy exclaimed. "Thanks, Mr. Johnson. You've given us a really helpful idea." At that the boys scurried off to the bee hives again.

"I found an ant!" exclaimed Jason. "See, it's a black one and it's walking toward the hives." The ant in question was about ten feet from the hive. Both boys watched anxiously as it slowly, yet persistently, moved through the grass. At first it seemed to be moving toward the bee hives. But when it got about a foot and a half away, it veered off and headed toward the woods.

"Too bad," Andy said. "I thought we were going to solve the mystery for sure that time. Let's see if we can find any more ants."

Indeed the boys were able to find a number of ants, as well as many other insects. In fact, they got so wrapped up in observing the insects, that for a time they forgot why they were watching them. Mom's voice from the house brought them back to their senses. They were being called in to lunch.

"Let's go," Jason said. "I don't think ants are our problem."

"I agree," Andy replied. "But we're not any closer to solving the Case of the Missing Bees."

"We'll just have to do more detective work later," was Jason's logical reply. After all, it was lunch time!

When Cathy entered the kitchen for lunch she said, "I was thinking. You know what it could be? Maybe it's ants! They do kill and carry off bees."

The boys grinned at each other. Correction: Jason grinned only for a second. "It's not ants," Andy said. "Mr. Johnson told us that might be the problem.

We've already checked it out. There are no ants climbing up into the hives or coming out. Also, there aren't any ants on the ground moving in the direction of the hives." Then he added, "I'm afraid we're stumped again."

Chapter Five

If the boys were sad about not solving the Case of the Missing Bees, you sure wouldn't be able to tell it from the way they ate. Today they had tuna, apples, fresh homemade bread, yogurt, and some dried banana strips.

After lunch, the boys never did get back to the bee hives. Actually, they didn't know what their next step should be. They had exhausted all of their possibilities and were waiting for some new clue to present itself.

The boys spent a good bit of the afternoon working on schoolwork. Mom gave them a history lesson to complete. Neither boy cared much for history. Jason had summed up the boys' feelings when he said to Andy, "History is about stuff that has already happened. Why should we care about what happened a long time ago? How is that going to help us today?" They were good boys, however, and didn't complain to Mom. They did their lessons. Yet, they didn't really enjoy the subject.

Before long, Dad was home and it was time for supper. How the boys enjoyed the supper conversation! Dad was always telling them about something that happened at work or some story from his childhood. Since Dad was a fork lift operator at a lumber mill, his stories were even more exciting to the boys.

The blessing was asked and everyone filled their plates. Dad winked at Mom and said, "It sure is a mystery to me." Then he looked at Ben and asked, "Can you pass the corn please?"

"What's a mystery?" asked Jason excitedly.

"Mystery?" Dad asked. "Oh, I was just saying it sure is a mystery to me. But it's a bigger and even more important mystery to John Popper, the owner of our mill. Cathy, can you pass the salt please?"

Dad waited a second to let the excitement and interest build before continuing. "John is one puzzled man," he began. "He came to me today and said he had a real mystery on his hands. I immediately told him that I knew of a detective agency that might be able to help solve it."

"Do you mean The Great Detective Agency?" Andy asked in disbelief.

"That's the only one we have, isn't it?" his father returned, smiling.

"What's the mystery, Dad?" Cathy questioned. Everyone was excited by now.

"Well, it appears that some gas is missing at the plant. We installed a three thousand-gallon propane tank in October. John took a measurement of it a few days ago and to the best of his knowledge he had lost about 250 gallons of the gas."

"Maybe he used it," Andy suggested, "and forgot that he had."

Dad buttered his corn and replied, "Maybe. Of course, the problem is that he keeps pretty good records of what gas is used. No, he is convinced that something or somebody has been stealing his gas."

"Did you say you told him about our detective agency?" Jason asked, trying to direct the conversation back to this important issue.

The Mysterious Message

"What I said was 'I know of a detective agency that might be able to help.' John replied to me, 'Timothy, I can't afford to hire a detective. It would cost too much money!' Naturally I told him that you guys work for free. That is still your policy, isn't it?"

"Yes sir!" Andy quickly said. "What did he say then?"

"He was amazed that anyone would do detective work for free. So, I explained who the owners of The Great Detective Agency were and he immediately seemed to understand things better. Anyway," Dad finished, "I promised him that I would tell you about the situation and see what you could come up with."

Jason and Andy were thrilled. Imagine! A real company that wanted **them** to help solve a mystery.

Jason tried his best to sound grown up and in control. "What are the facts, Dad? Start from the beginning if you don't mind." Needless to say, both Jason's and Andy's spiral notebooks were in hand as this question was posed.

Dad filled them in on the facts. "The tank is above ground and is brand new. It would be surprising if it has any leaks. In fact, part of the installation process included a number of tests to make sure there were no leaks. It was filled on October 15, right after it was delivered and installed."

"What do you use the gas for, Dad?" Andy asked.

"Well, we use a small amount of propane to run our fork lifts. We have a number of heaters at the mill, too. Of course, the kiln uses more propane than anything else. John is pretty cost-conscious and installed usage meters on things that are hooked up directly to the tank. When he compared his usage with what is left in the tank, he was off by over two hundred gallons. You guys think about that mystery and see what you can come up with, okay? I promise to relay any information you give me directly to John."

"Can we go to the mill, Dad?" asked Jason. "It would·make it easier to check for clues."

Dad looked at Mom. There was some subtle nonverbal communication between the two. Then Dad answered, smiling, "No, I guess this is one case you are going to have to solve 'long distance.' Just think about it and see what you can come up with."

The boys asked a few more questions but soon supper was declared "over" by Mom. "Honestly, I think you boys would eat nonstop, around the clock if I would let you," she said, smiling. She loved to see them eat her cooking. "You need to get your evening chores done quickly. I want you to get baths tonight."

Right before family devotions that evening, the boys met in their cramped office under the basement stairs. "Any ideas?" asked Jason.

"All I can think of is that someone drove in and stole it, or else the tank has some kind of a leak," Andy replied honestly. "Yet, Dad said neither was very likely. The plant is fenced and locked up at night. There was no evidence that anyone had messed with the fence. Also, the tank was checked for leaks by the gas company when they installed it and they guaranteed that no leaks were present. If we can trust both of those statements as facts, then I don't know what else it could be."

"Me neither," said Jason. "But we won't give up! We'll keep thinking until we come up with some ideas. Now we have something else neat to work on tomorrow. Things are really looking up for The Great Detective Agency!"

"Boys, time for devotions," Dad called from the top of the steps. As the family gathered in the living room, Dad closed a magazine he had been reading and picked up his Bible.

He read from Ephesians 4:17-29, a passage which was a little hard to understand until Dad explained it to them. "It is important for Christians to live differently from the rest of the world," he warned. "We must give up all of the sins that we sometimes want to hang onto. Things like lying, anger, stealing, and saying evil things. The Bible says that we certainly didn't learn these things from Christ! Instead, we are to tell the truth. And we are supposed to work with our hands, so that we will have money to give to those who are needy."

After making sure that everyone understood the verses, Dad picked up the prayer calendar and read the entry for that day. "Before we pray," Dad added, "I would like to relate a story I just read. He held up the magazine he had been reading and continued. "Some years ago, Christians were able to give Bibles to Russian soldiers, even though the authorities were watching carefully to make sure this didn't happen. Remember, this is a true story. These Christians would go to railroad stations which were filled with Russian soldiers. In fact, soldiers were the only ones allowed to ride the trains at that time. Anyway, these Christians would position themselves near the end of the train, and pretend to just be looking at the soldiers. As the train started to pull out of the station, these Christians would take Bibles from where they had hidden them in their clothing, and toss them through the open windows of the train. The soldiers aboard the train gladly grabbed the Bibles." Jason sat up straighter in his chair and smiled. This was a good story.

"However," Dad continued, "the Russian secret police, who were riding up with the engineer in the front of the train, saw what was going on and started shouting angrily. As the train continued to pull out of the station, the leaders would quickly begin making their way through the train cars toward the back of the train. Meanwhile, the Russian soldiers, who didn't want to give up their new treasures, would walk forward a few train cars and trade seats with other soldiers. By the time the leaders had made it all the way to the back of the train and searched it carefully, there were no Bibles to be found! Those Christians at the train station literally risked their lives to get Bibles into the hungry hands of the soldiers."

"They were very brave!" Andy exclaimed.

"Yes, they were," Dad agreed. "It is the Holy Spirit which helped them to be so brave. We need to have the same conviction and attitude. As we pray for the persecuted church tonight, let's also ask God to help us to be brave for Christ."

"You mean like Ronco, don't you Dad?" Ben asked.

"Yes son, that's right. Actually, his name is Marco, but God knows who you're praying for." The family had been praying for a man named Marco who was in a Cuban prison for telling others about Jesus inside his own house.

After prayers, the boys went to their room. As

they were getting into bed, Ben spoke up. "Mom, I have some stuff in my throat when I swallow. What should I do?"

"Why don't you try getting a drink of water and see if that helps?" she offered.

A few minutes later, Mom stopped Ben who was starting to race down the stairs. "Hold on there, buddy! Where are you heading?" she asked.

"I need to go tell Daddy something."

"Can't it wait until tomorrow? It's very late," Mom said, looking at the clock on the wall.

"I need to tell him that if he ever gets gunk in his throat, that taking a drink of water will help!" he said excitedly.

"I think that's something that can wait until tomorrow," Mom instructed, leading Ben back to his room and his bed.

As she kissed the boys and started to turn out the lights, Ben's disappointed voice could be heard. "Well, I guess I also need to tell Daddy that it will only help for a **minute**." Soon all was quiet and the boys were sleeping peacefully.

Chapter Six

Wake up, Andy! Wake up, Jason! It's snowing!" Ben shouted in delight early on Wednesday morning.

Jason was out of bed before Andy. "Ben, you're probably confused. It must be fog . . . hey Andy! It **is** snowing!" he enthused.

Andy stretched, trying to understand why his pastor was reciting a poem to him about snow. As his mind cleared, and the dream slowly slid away to wherever dreams go, he too jumped up and ran to the window. There was no doubt. That white stuff gently falling from the sky was snow! It looked like there was already maybe an inch on the ground. "Hooray!" he exclaimed, perhaps more loudly than he should have indoors.

"Boys!" Mom's voice could be heard as she moved up the stairs. "Boys, I've told you not to shout in the house."

"We're sorry, Mom," the three boys said. Then Jason added, "I know we shouldn't shout and I'm really sorry. I guess when I saw the snow I just forgot everything."

Mom was in their doorway by this time. "I know it's exciting, guys. I forgive all of you. Now, get dressed quickly and come on down. Breakfast will be ready soon. The blueberry muffins are just about ready to come out of the oven." With that, the rustle

The Mysterious Message

of Mom's dress could be heard as she descended the stairs.

Quickly, for there were muffins **and** snow to contend with this morning, the boys dressed, made their beds, and put away their night clothes. Dad and Cathy were already at the table. Cathy's eyes were sparkling. She loved snow as much as the boys did. Although it usually did snow at least once a year where the Nelsons lived, it was still an unusual enough occurrence to bring a level of delight that Midwestern children could never understand.

"So what are you going to do today?" Dad asked no one in particular after the blessing was finished.

Most eyes were on Mom. Not that she was going to be the one to play in the snow all day. No, they looked at her because she decided when homeschooling would take place and when "recess" would occur. The many sets of pleading eyes caused her to get tickled and she almost choked on a muffin. After taking a drink of milk, she said, "Well, the snow won't last too long, you know. It is so early in the year and it's been so warm that I doubt it will be here much past lunch." She looked at the boys. "Do you think you made good progress in your lessons yesterday?" she asked seriously.

Jason looked down and started to blush. He couldn't help remembering how he and Andy had gotten sidetracked and goofed off when they should have been doing their school work. If he had only known it was going to snow today . . .

Andy, too, realized the lesson Mom was trying to give them.

Mom let them ponder over this for a few minutes

37

before stating, "I think they can go outside right after breakfast for a few hours. But then I expect them to work extra hard later today. Do you think that's possible, boys?" Mom asked, smiling at the now-happy faces.

"Yes ma'am!" they replied. Then Andy said, "I think I should do my work well every day. You never know what might come up on the next day."

"That's true, of course," Dad said. "Actually, you should do your work well every day because that is what is pleasing to the Lord. You remember our memory verse. Colossians 3:23. Let's all say it together."

The family spoke in unison: "And whatsoever ye do, do it heartily, as to the Lord, and not unto men."

Then on a lighter note Dad added, "I hope you all have fun. I remember how much fun I had as a boy in the snow."

"I don't think you have to worry about them having fun, Timothy," Mom smiled.

After breakfast, the boys had to waste precious time desperately searching for their gloves. Five minutes after walking down the stairs to the basement, the boys had found only 1 ½ pair. "Has anyone seen my other glove?" asked Jason frantically.

"I think Ben was using it to be an airplane pilot last summer," Andy said. "Ben, do you know where Jason's other glove is?"

"No, I don't think I even remember using it," Ben answered. "I'm going to make a big snowman."

"I'm not sure there will be enough snow for a snowman, Ben. But we'll see . . . hey! Here it is!" said Jason. He was lying on his stomach, using the handle of a broom to pull things out from under the dryer. Along with the broom came a bunch of lint, an old pop bottle cap, several empty shotgun shells, a collection of rocks, small change, and his other glove.

"You found my bottle cap!" Ben exclaimed with delight. "Thanks!"

Ben's gloves could not be found anywhere. Finally, Andy ran to ask Mom if she could help find them. "Oh, I'm sorry," Mom said. "I threw them away after last winter. There wasn't much left of them after having been handed down so many times. I've got a new pair for him here in the closet." Taking the gloves, Andy raced back down the stairs.

"Oh! They're beautiful!" said Ben admiringly, as he pulled the gloves onto his hands.

"Let's go!" said Jason, leading the way up the basement steps and out the back door.

It was still snowing softly. The sky didn't give any indication that it would end anytime soon. "Maybe the weather man will be wrong and it will snow all week!" Jason hoped out loud.

The boys had fun running and sliding in the white landscape. Jason asked Mom for an old cookie sheet which the boys used to "sled" down a hill beside the house. After a while, they started walking around their farm, trying to make unusual tracks in the snow. Andy found that he could keep one foot facing forward and one facing backwards as he walked. It made quite a confusing set of tracks for anyone who might happen by later!

Without planning to do it, the boys ended up near the bee hives. Ben noticed them first. "Look, Andy! There are tracks to the bee hives."

Sure enough, there were several sets of small tracks leading to the bee hives. "Hey Jason," Andy said. "What do you think?"

"They are tracks all right," he agreed. "And they lead right up to the hives' entrance. I wonder what kind of tracks they are."

"Let's run and get our book on mammals and see if we can figure them out," Andy suggested as he turned to head back to the house. A few minutes later the boys were studying the tracks and turning pages in the book.

"I think it is kind of like this one," Ben said time and again, trying to help, but pointing out just about every animal in the book.

After studying the tracks more carefully, Jason concluded, "It looks like they were made by a skunk. Too bad. That really doesn't help us understand what has been happening to the bees. I can't see an old smelly skunk killing a bunch of bees. Can you?"

Andy and Ben both laughed. "No," Andy said. "I guess the bees would fly the other way when a skunk got close." Then as if it were necessary to explain what he meant, he held his nose and made a face.

"Well, we'll just have to keep thinking. It's too bad they weren't bear tracks," Jason remarked, turning back to the house. "We better put this book away before we start playing again."

As they got to the house, the boys were surprised to learn that it was almost lunch time. "How can it be?" asked Andy. "We just got out here."

Only when they were in the house did the boys realize how wet their gloves and pants were. It felt good to sit down to a hot bowl of Mom's soup.

Chapter Seven

After lunch, the boys worked on their lessons. They were diligent this time, not attempting to goof off or play around. The close call this morning of possibly missing out on getting to go outside had reminded them that they should always obey their parents and work hard.

In the middle of the afternoon, the phone rang. "Oh, and look at my hands," Mom said out loud. She was patting out some dough for a treat after supper and her hands were covered in flour. "Can one of you boys get the phone?"

Ben was standing in the kitchen and asked, "Can I please answer it, Mom?"

"Sure," Mom said. "Just remember to say 'Hello' this time." She remembered how Ben had forgotten to make that simple statement when he had picked up the phone the last time, which resulted in the person on the other end hanging up. They never did figure out who had called.

"Hello," Ben said politely and clearly as he picked up the receiver. His shining eyes were sparkling at his mom as he listened to what the other party was saying. Then, Ben responded to the caller with "Yes, she's home. Goodbye." He quickly replaced the receiver on the hook and turned to walk out of the kitchen. He was obviously pleased with himself.

Mom called out quickly, "Well, who was it, Ben?

What did they want?"

"I don't know," he answered. "They just asked if you were home. I told them 'Yes' and then I hung up." That didn't sound right. He thought a second, then added, "Oh, I told them 'Goodbye' also."

Mom started to sigh, but just then the phone rang again. "Want me to get that?" Ben asked.

"No thanks, Ben," Mom reassured him, moving toward the phone. "I think I can get it now."

Late in the afternoon, Mom surprised the boys again. "How would you like to go outside for a while? You've really made good progress this afternoon on your lessons."

The boys didn't have to be asked twice. Even though their gloves were still a little damp inside, they didn't complain. Nor did they complain that it was no longer snowing. They were just happy that the snow was still on the ground and that they could go out and enjoy it.

According to Mom, the weather man had changed the forecast. The snow was supposed to all melt by later that night, and in this part of Tennessee one never knew when the next snow might come, if at all, this year.

Ben, Jason, and Andy decided to take a walk through their woods. Since Mom had said it was okay ("Just don't run off and leave Ben behind"), off they went. As they walked, the boys talked about the Case of the Missing Gas.

"With all the excitement of the snow, I had totally forgotten it," admitted Andy.

"Me too," confessed Jason. "Well, do you have

any ideas?"

No one spoke as they continued to walk through the fluffy snow. It was hard to believe that the four inches of snow would be gone by tomorrow morning. "I still think it's possible that someone stole the gas," Andy said.

Jason thought about that possibility. "Yes, that's what keeps going through my mind, too. Dad seemed so sure that it couldn't be that. But sometimes, the thing that no one expects is exactly what the solution is."

"Wouldn't it be possible for someone, if they had a key to the lock on the gate, to unlock the gate, steal the gas, and then lock it back up as they left? If they did that, then no one would suspect them."

"Makes sense to me. Only problem is, where could they get a key?" Jason questioned.

"The hardware store sells keys. I've seen them," Ben offered. "I even saw a man buying one!" he concluded in an awed voice, as though this purchase was very mysterious, and perhaps even the solution to the Case of the Missing Gas.

Jason threw a stick up high into a tree, trying to get the snow to fall down. He was very successful: all the boys' clothes were now covered with snow. "Sure they sell them, Ben. But you have to have a key first for them to make a copy of it. You can't just go in and ask to buy a key for a lock without having a key already yourself."

Ben didn't seem convinced by this information. "Well, I saw him buying one!" he repeated with importance.

"I wonder how many men at the mill have a key to

the gate?" Andy mused. "There must be several men who have keys, and if we can just find out —"

Jason wondered why Andy had stopped talking so abruptly. Turning, he found Andy staring at the path ahead. Jason's eyes followed Andy's gaze toward the ground, then he too stopped and stared.

Ben, not paying much attention to what was going on, was chattering something to himself about finding keys in the basement. He accidently ran right into Jason's still figure. "Oh! Why'd you stop?" he wondered out loud.

Normally Jason would have tried to correct Ben and tell him that he should say "I'm sorry" when you bump into people accidently. But not today. Not right now. He was too busy trying to take in the scene in front of him. Andy too, stooping down, was studying the situation carefully.

"I wonder who made that?" Andy finally said.

"Beats me," Jason said. "At first I thought it must have been made by Cathy. I thought that she might have taken a walk down this path this morning. Then I remembered that our tracks were the first ones in the snow from the house to here." He leaned down to look at the writing in the snow.

"What does it say?" asked Ben. He was learning his letters, but still had trouble reading most words.

Andy stood back up and looked around into the surrounding woods. It seemed darker than it had just minutes before. Looking at Ben he said quietly, "All it says is 'I will see you Sat.' I wonder what that means?"

Jason didn't answer. He was looking beyond the writing that was so clearly visible at the edge of the snowy path to a heap beneath the snow. "Look, Andy. Here's something else. I don't remember this pile of rocks being here. Do you?"

"I'm sure that wasn't there before!" Andy had a sudden thought. "Hey Jason," he said quickly. "With this snow we should be able to track this person and see where he came from!"

Ben wasn't so sure he wanted to do that. He sensed the excitement and fear in his brothers' voices. "I'm . . . I'm a little afraid," he stammered. "I think I want to go home now."

"But Ben," Jason pleaded, "what if the tracks are gone by the time we get back? Don't you want to solve this mystery and see who wrote that?"

"Not really," Ben answered. Ben was a very practical little boy.

"I'll tell you what," Andy coaxed. "If you'll come with us, I'll hold your hand. How about that?"

Ben thought about that possibility. After a minute he agreed. "Okay, but I may get afraid even with your hand," he warned.

"If you do, you just tell us and we'll go back home," Jason promised.

The boys moved forward and studied a fresh set of tracks in the snow.

Chapter Eight

The tracks were made by a boot and were larger than their own boot prints. "Must be an older boy," Jason guessed.

"Yes, or a man," Andy assented. Then remembering that he should try to keep Ben from getting scared, he added in a more cheerful voice, "It's probably just some neighbor. Let's go see."

The boys followed the tracks along the path. It was easy to see that someone had walked to where the words were written in the snow and then turned and walked back. At places it looked like the person had tried to lead the boys off the path. The boot prints would leave the trail at these places and walk around a tree or behind a rock. Once, the person had apparently even climbed a tree and then jumped from a low limb.

"What do you think?" asked Jason. "Is he trying to lose us?"

"I don't know," Andy said. "Hey, what's this?"

The boys stopped again. Here was more writing in the soft snow. This time it said, "Good job!"

"That couldn't have been written long ago or it would have been buried in the snowfall," Jason noted. "I suspect it was written no more than one hour ago." That thought sobered both older boys. They looked carefully in the surrounding woods.

"Think the person could have backtracked and still

The Mysterious Message

be around here somewhere?" Andy whispered to Jason as they stooped to look at the message.

"I don't know," Jason whispered back, looking at one oak tree again and again. Was that a shadow behind the tree? Or could it be part of a man's black jacket showing beyond the edge of the tree? Jason wanted to know. Yet, in some ways he didn't want to know, either.

The boys were very excited by this time and walked a little faster. Before long, however, they reached the edge of the woods that marked the border of their property. The boot prints continued, however, past their property line.

"Should we keep tracking him?" asked Andy.

"No way," Jason said. "You know Mom and Dad said we can't leave our property without their permission. And here's Dad's sign, easy to see." Dad had erected a red sign several years ago to warn the boys that they had reached their farm's limits. The sign read "WHOA! Best stop here guys!!"

The boys had no choice but to turn and walk back to the house. They studied the clues as they passed them again. Their minds were racing, trying to figure out what this new mystery meant. When they got home, they told their mom all about it. At first she seemed alarmed. When they related what the words said, however, she seemed to lose her anxiety. "I guess that's a mystery for The Great Detective Agency," she decided.

"Aren't you worried?" asked Jason.

"No, I think you can handle that mystery," Mom answered with a smile. "I would recommend you keep hunting for clues."

Jason and Andy were surprised and perplexed by Mom's comments and her attitude. It was obvious to them that someone had entered their property, left a message that didn't make any sense to them, and left again. Why wouldn't she be concerned about that?

"Mom, did you leave those messages?" Andy asked, thinking he had solved the mystery.

Mom laughed out loud. "No boys, I've been busy making gingerbread cookies this afternoon. Want one?"

The boys couldn't resist that offer. And the more they questioned Mom, the more convinced they became that she had nothing to do with the Case of the Mysterious Message.

When Dad came home from work, the boys quickly filled him in on the details. Watching him carefully as they gave him this information, neither boy felt that Dad had anything to do with the mysterious messages. Cathy was not "guilty" either.

As the food was passed at supper, Dad began to tell what had happened at the lumber mill that day. "The snow created some excitement for me today. I was hauling some logs with my fork lift when a delivery truck suddenly came around the corner of the building. I slammed on my brakes, but that snow made the ground so slippery that I just slid for several feet. I must have hit some pavement or something, because the fork lift suddenly came to an abrupt stop. That jerking stop caused two large logs to fall off my lift and start rolling right for the delivery van. I'm talking about BIG logs, too." Dad paused to pass the milk to Ben. Everyone was listening carefully for Dad to continue telling his story.

The Mysterious Message

"It's hard to believe, but that delivery man acted like nothing was happening. I don't know. Maybe he didn't see the trouble I was having. Anyway, while all of that was happening to me, he had been finding the package he was going to deliver and was just stepping out of his van when he looked forward and saw the logs rolling right for him. I don't know when I've seen anyone move so fast! He jumped back in his van and tried to start the engine. It wouldn't start. He looked up at me with a look of disbelief on his face.

"The logs kept rolling, although slower by now. There sure wasn't anything I could do but sit there and watch. Right before the first one was going to hit the delivery van, it stopped. Just like that," he said, snapping his fingers. A general sigh of relief could be felt around the table.

"Then what happened?" asked Andy.

"The driver seemed to regain his composure pretty quickly. I guess those guys have to get used to delivering in some pretty scary situations. By the time I got off my fork lift and started walking to his van, he was already out walking toward me with a package. After talking to him a minute, and apologizing, I offered to take the package from him. As I was walking toward the office with the package, I happened to glance at the box. Guess what it was?"

Several people tried to guess. Jason thought it was brake parts for the fork lift. Andy thought it was some bearings for one of the machines. Ben thought it was some doughnuts. "Nope," Dad said to each attempt. "Give up?" Soon everyone did.

"Ladies' slippers!" Dad laughed. "I don't know if the driver just got confused by what all had happened,

49

but he delivered one case of Marson's assorted ladies' slippers to our lumber mill. You can imagine the funny jokes everyone told all day!"

Later, as the supper conversation died down some, Jason felt like he just had to ask a question. "Are you all sure that you have nothing at all to do with the messages out in the snow?" Everyone at the table denied any conspiracy in the case. "Well, Andy," he concluded, "I guess we really do have another mystery on our hands now!"

"Speaking of mysteries," Dad said. "The mystery at work is solved." Everyone stopped eating.

"Today," Dad continued, "John told me that he finally had it figured out. You see . . ." Dad had planned to tell his family the solution to the mystery. But seeing the interested faces around the table, he decided on a different course altogether. "Actually, I think I would like to give you all some more time to see if you can solve it," he said with a twinkle in his eye. "Have you any new ideas?" he asked, looking directly at the older boys.

"Sorry, Dad. I guess we were too busy playing in the snow," admitted Andy.

"That's okay," Dad returned. "I'll tell you how we'll do this. Every night at supper time you can ask me four questions about the Case of the Missing Gas. I'll answer them and we'll see how long it will take you to solve the mystery. Does that sound like fun?"

"Yes!" the boys agreed. Even Mom and Cathy seemed interested.

"So, tell me about your day in the snow," Dad prompted. Soon all mysteries were forgotten as the children related their joys of the day.

The Mysterious Message

After family devotions, the boys walked to their bedroom. "Four questions," mused Jason. "I guess I know what we'll be doing tomorrow."

Andy agreed. "This should be fun. Of course, we still have the Case of the Missing Bees, and the Case of the Mysterious Message to work on as well. Even without snow, I can't wait for tomorrow!"

Chapter Nine

Before Andy woke up on Wednesday morning, he was having a delightful dream about sledding down a steep hill with snow flying in his face. A dog was running along beside him, somehow keeping up with the racing sled. "Come on, boy!" Andy called to the dog. Misunderstanding Andy, the dog jumped right onto the sled and the two raced the rest of the way down the hill. As he got near the bottom, he heard Jason call from behind him, "Hey you better . . ." Andy couldn't tell what else Jason said because the sled upset at that time, with the dog and Andy rolling over and over in the soft snow. Once again, Andy heard Jason. "Andy, you better get up."

Andy raised his head to find Jason looking down at Andy in his bed. At first Andy was a little confused. Then he realized the sledding had been just a dream. *Too bad*, Andy thought. Then he remembered that they really did have snow and he struggled to untangle himself from the covers in order to look out the window.

Before he reached the window, though, Jason announced, sadly, "It's pretty much all gone, Andy. That's the first thing I looked for this morning too."

Jason was right. But how could almost all of that snow disappear overnight? It probably turned warm, just like the weatherman had predicted. Sure enough, there were puddles forming in the yard where the boys had so much fun yesterday.

The Mysterious Message

Andy was normally a cheerful boy. Yet, as he came down the stairs and into the kitchen, Mom noticed his downcast eyes and sad expression. Andy walked over to the kitchen window, looked out, then sighed loudly. Plopping down in a chair, Andy blurted out, "Mom, why can't we have more snow? Why did it all have to go away last night?"

Mom walked over and placed her hands on Andy's shoulders. She gently rubbed his shoulders before turning his face up to look into hers. "Andy, I know how disappointed you are. I'm sorry that you won't be able to play in the snow today."

"I know, Mom," Andy said. "But it's not your fault."

Mom thought about that and decided to have a little talk with Andy. "I'm not sure 'fault' is a good word to use in this case, Andy. Whose 'fault' is it that the snow is gone today? Who made the weather get warmer so that the snow melted last night? Whose 'fault' is it that you had snow to play in yesterday?"

Andy felt a little guilty. "I guess God made the weather warmer."

"That's right," Mom agreed, rubbing Andy's shoulders again. "I know how easy it is to complain about the weather. It seems that almost everyone does! I've been guilty of it. But I am getting more and more convinced that we have no right to complain to God about the weather. Also, it seems to me that we should remember to thank Him when He kindly sends us snow to play in. What do you think?"

Andy nodded. "You're right," he said. "I remember that verse . . . you know, the one we learned that said that all things work out for our good if we are

Christians." Andy straightened up in his chair. "I guess that goes for the weather too."

Mom gave him one last rub and walked back to the stove. As she finished making the preparations for breakfast, she thanked God that Andy was maturing so much. *Please help him to continue to seek Your face for wisdom and knowledge*, she silently prayed.

After breakfast, Mom gave all the children their assignments for the morning. Cathy continued to work on a blouse she was making for the next summer. She also worked on a composition that she planned to submit to one of the magazines she subscribed to called *Future Homemakers*. The boys worked on math problems and some spelling words.

At about 11:00, Mom announced that it was time for a break.

"Should we get our snow clothes on?" questioned Ben.

"No, I guess we won't need those today," Jason replied. "There's not enough snow to play in."

"What will we do, then?" Ben asked.

"Now that's a good question. Say, maybe we can go back to the woods and look at the clues again for the Case of the Mysterious Message. Maybe there are more clues that were under the snow somehow. Ben, do you want to go or just play here near the house?" Andy asked, pulling on a pair of rubbers.

Ben thought for a minute. "I don't know."

When they went outside, Ben placed himself near a puddle and began shoveling the little snow that was left into the water. "I'm going to stay here," he announced to his brothers.

Jason and Andy walked down the path that

wound through the woods. It was hard to believe that just yesterday everything had been covered with a layer of white. They talked about the cases they were working on.

"We need to come up with four questions for the Case of the Missing Gas," Jason reminded Andy. "Dad said we could ask him four questions tonight. Wouldn't it be neat to ask questions that would solve it **tonight**?"

"Sure, but what should we ask?" Andy queried.

The two walked in silence for a minute. "I think we should ask who has a key to the gate," Andy finally decided.

"Yes, I do too," Jason agreed. "We probably should also find out if the gas somehow reappeared. You know Dad said that the mystery had been solved. He didn't tell us how it was solved. Maybe it was just a mistake on Mr. Popper's part, and there never was any gas missing."

"That's a good idea," Andy responded. "Well, that's two questions we can ask." Rather than thinking of more questions, however, the boys suddenly became silent. They were approaching the bend in the trail where the mysterious message had been placed yesterday.

Most of the snow was gone. Thus, the writing had all but disappeared. The only impressions left in the snow were portions of some of the letters. "I think this is the bottom part of the 'S'," Andy said.

"The pile of rocks is still here," noted Jason. Then stooping down he started to toss the rocks away.

"Hey, what are you doing?" asked Andy.

"I'm moving these rocks. Maybe there is a mes-

The Farm Mystery Series

sage under them. Why else would someone make a pile of rocks?" But after moving all the rocks, there was no message or further clue to be found. Just some cold, damp earth.

The boys then looked around the area more closely. "Nothing else," Jason acknowledged sadly. "I don't see anything, do you?"

"No. Why don't we walk down the path some more?" Andy suggested. "Maybe we'll see something that we missed yesterday because of the snow." The boys began to walk again, paying careful attention to every detail around them. Their level of attention precluded any conversation between them. There was a tenseness in their walking. An anticipation of something coming up ahead. What could it be? Were they ready for whatever it was?

After walking a while, Jason, especially, seemed more relaxed. Finally he stopped. "Do you think we need to go any further?" he asked. "Seems like we would have seen something by now."

"We might as well walk to Dad's sign at the edge of our property," Andy suggested. At that, the boys began walking again. After going around two bends in the trail, they suddenly stopped.

A small tree was blocking their path. There was no way that it could have just fallen into that position. It looked as though it had been purposefully placed in order to obstruct their path. The tree was lying at about a 45-degree angle from the ground on the right side of the path up to a tree on the left side of the path. Kneeling down, Andy announced the verdict that both boys suspected. "It was cut, Jason!"

Chapter Ten

Jason got down and looked at the tree. "Looks like they used a saw," he added. "It's a clean cut, not like one made by a hatchet or ax. But why was it cut? When could they have cut it?" He looked around into the surrounding woods, a tense feeling returning. "And who did it?"

Both boys were solemn as they carefully searched for more clues. They didn't find anything on the ground or on the sapling itself. Then for some reason Andy's eyes followed the sapling up into the tree it was leaning on. "What's that?" he asked, pointing to a piece of cardboard attached with string to a limb halfway up the tree. Without answering, Jason began climbing up to retrieve the piece of cardboard. He looked at it, dropped it down to Andy, then climbed back down to the ground. Andy picked up the cardboard and read it:

> So we meet again! I know about you two. But what do you know about me? Better start learning. Sat is coming soon!

"What's going on?" Andy asked. "Who is this guy? And how are we supposed to learn about him?" Andy was thinking out loud and didn't expect his brother to be able to answer these questions. Perhaps it was for that reason that he jumped when Jason answered.

"Beats me, Andy! This is very strange," Jason replied. "I don't know anyone our age around here who could have done this. Jerry lives over four miles from here. And Matt is only seven. I doubt he would do this."

"'Sat is coming soon.' Whoever is writing this expects something to happen Saturday. At least, I assume that is what Sat stands for," Andy commented. "When we get home, we can look it up in the dictionary. Maybe it also stands for something else."

"Yes, like satellite or something," said Jason. "I'll let you look that up and report when we meet this afternoon, okay?" Andy nodded. "Let's see if there are any more clues here."

Both boys craned their necks looking up and down all the trees in the area. They looked on the ground, under rocks, and behind trees. When they were both convinced that there was nothing else to find, Jason spoke. "Well, I guess we might as well head back toward the house. It's probably time for us to go in anyway."

As the boys passed near the bee hives, they couldn't resist taking a quick look to see if anything had changed. They found everything as it should be. A few bees were out this morning, perhaps because the weather had warmed up so much. Still, there seemed to be little activity. "I wonder if we've lost any more bees," worried Andy. "We can't forget the Case of the Missing Bees, Jason."

"I know," Jason agreed. "Let's talk about that when we meet. Maybe we can ask Mom if she has any ideas. Why don't you ask her?"

The Mysterious Message

After lunch, the boys got back to their lessons. In mid-afternoon, Mom dismissed lessons for the day. Andy and Jason quickly made their way to the office of The Great Detective Agency under the basement stairs.

"Why don't we take one case at a time and see where we are on it?" Jason suggested.

"Well, we have the Case of the Missing Bees," said Andy. "I did remember to ask Mom if she had any ideas. She didn't."

"We know it's probably not ants. Or disease. And it's not because they have flown away in a swarm. What do you think we should do now?" asked Jason.

Andy thought about it for a minute. "I don't know. I hate to tell Cathy that we're quitting on the job, though. I just don't know what else to do."

"Maybe we should start looking at the hives more often. How about first thing in the morning, right before lunch, and after we do the evening chores? We can see if we notice anything out of the ordinary each time and keep a record. Other than that, I don't know what we can do either," Jason concluded.

"I agree," Andy said. "I'll be sure and look first thing each morning, you look after you do the evening chores, and we'll look together right before lunch. Does that seem fair?"

"Sounds good, partner," Jason smiled. "Now, what about the Case of the Missing Gas? We have two questions already. What should our other two questions be?"

"Why don't we ask Dad if it is possible that someone drove in during the day and stole some gas? You know, maybe with all the saws running it was so noisy that they didn't notice someone driving in and filling up a tank," Andy said.

"But how could they steal that much gas?" Jason asked.

"I don't know. Maybe they stole it over several weeks' time. Yes, maybe that is it. Someone could have come in at the same time every day, while the mill was running loudly, and stolen gas each time," Andy suggested.

"Okay, I agree that's a good question to ask. We still have one more to ask." Both boys sat deep in thought. The only sound to be heard for several minutes was the washing machine as it went through a rinse and spin cycle. When the washing machine finally stopped spinning, the silence was almost uncomfortable. As a result the boys started talking to fill the airwaves with something.

"Boy, I'm having trouble coming up with another one, how about you, Jason?" asked Andy.

"Well, I have one, but I'm not sure how strong it is," Jason answered reluctantly. "I wonder if it is possible that Mr. Popper stole the gas himself, but pretended that someone else stole it. Maybe to collect the insurance on it or something. What do you think?"

Andy would have laughed if Ben had made this suggestion. But since it was his partner, he restrained himself. "Jason, why in the world would Mr. Popper steal his own gas and then tell everyone that it was missing? Besides, I don't think that Mr. Popper would do something like that. Dad always talks about him like he is a nice man. I think he's a Christian."

"Maybe you're right, Andy. It's just that I've heard of people who pretended to be good, but who were actually doing something very bad. Sometimes it takes years for someone to find out what they're doing. And all the time, they have been fooling people into thinking they are good people."

"Wow." Andy was visibly impressed. He did not remember ever having heard of things like that. "I guess that's a possibility then. Sure, let's go ahead and ask Dad that also. So, it looks like we have our four questions. Good!"

Both boys were happy to have accomplished something on one of their cases. Not that they had solved it. They were just glad that they didn't have to think about that case again, at least until supper. That gave them time to devote all of their energy to the other cases pending.

"Now, what about the Case of the Mysterious Message?" asked Andy.

"Well, let's look at our clues," Jason said. The boys reviewed the facts they had recorded in their spiral notebooks. Then Andy picked up the piece of cardboard with the latest message on it and examined it closely.

It was an ordinary piece of cardboard that had been cut out of a larger piece of cardboard. Someone had used a dull instrument, like a knife or scissors, to cut out the piece. The writing was done with a red marking pen. Turning the clue over, Andy exclaimed, "Look, Jason! This was cut out of something that had printing on it! It has the letters 'Del' on it. And there are these two splotches of color on the left side of the letters. The top color is blue, the bottom is red."

Jason studied the cardboard more closely. "Yes, and you can just barely see part of the next letter after the 'l.' Most of it was cut off when the cardboard was cut down to make our note." All that was left of the next letter was a straight line, and the boys thought it was probably an 'i' or an 'l'. It could have been a 't' or an 'f' however. The piece of cardboard looked somewhat old and used. It was dirty on the side where the letters 'Del' were listed.

"I wonder what 'Del' stands for?" asked Andy. "I know it's just the first letters of something, but what? Do you remember seeing a box with something like that on it?"

Jason scratched his head. "For some reason it looks familiar," he replied. "Now, where have I seen it before?"

But try as they might, neither boy could remember what the 'Del' might stand for. Could it be the first part of a company's name? Or was it perhaps part of some instructions that were printed on a box, like 'LIVE FISH — Deliver As Soon As Possible!'? And what could the colors to the left of the letters represent?

"What about the handwriting?" Jason asked, trying to give his mind a rest from thinking of the letters 'Del.' "Would you say they were written by a man or a woman?"

"Looks like a guy's handwriting to me," Andy answered quickly. "It's pretty messy. Like yours and mine."

"Yes, I think so, too," Jason agreed. "Okay, for now, let's refer to this person as a 'he' until and unless we find some clue to make us think it's a female."

"Why is he doing this?" Andy asked the obvious question. Neither boy had any good ideas.

The Mysterious Message

"Maybe he's trying to scare us," Jason suggested. "I doubt it though," he continued almost immediately. "If he were trying to scare us, he could think of lots more scary messages to leave us than he has."

"On the other hand, maybe it's someone who needs help," Andy pondered. Then after further reflection, he added, "No. If he needs help, I don't think he would waste so much time and be so mysterious about it. Unless the help he needs is not right away. I mean maybe he doesn't need us right now, but he wants to make contact every day just in case he does need help in the near future."

"I think that it is just one of our friends who is trying to have fun with us," Jason said. The boys spent the next ten minutes discussing the boys who lived close enough to leave the clues.

They then talked about all the people who owned property adjacent to their farm. The most obvious would be Mr. Cartwright, who owned the land where the tracks continued past Dad's sign. But Mr. Cartwright was a bachelor in his 80's. No, it didn't seem like something he would do. In the end, they both agreed that it just couldn't be anyone who lived nearby.

"Well, I wonder if it could be a boy a little older than us?" Andy puzzled. "It just has to be, doesn't it?"

Jason thought about it. "Maybe," he said, hesitantly. "But there aren't any older children who live on farms near us either. Jeff Smith would have to come from over a mile away to do it. And Adam Claymore lives at least a mile and a half away. Do you really think they would walk that far each night just to do this?"

Both boys sat in thought for a moment. "You know," Jason remembered, breaking the silence, "Mom sure did seem a little funny when we told her about this yesterday. Do you think it's really her and she is just playing with us?"

"I don't think so," Andy shook his head. "I'll believe Mom. She said she didn't have anything to do with it. She's never told us a lie. I can't believe she would now."

"Me either," Jason admitted. "I was just trying to think of every possible angle. Well, it looks like we need to keep checking in the woods to see if there are any new clues." After a few seconds he added, "He came two days and left messages for us both days. If that is any indication, he should be back tomorrow sometime. Maybe we should try to go down that path several times a day just to figure out when he is coming. Who knows, we might even see him leaving a message. Wouldn't that be interesting?"

"Interesting, yes," Andy agreed. "But until I know who it is and why he is leaving those messages, I'm not real excited about running into him in our woods, a long way away from our house."

"You know, for some reason I'm not really afraid," Jason said. "I guess it's because Mom didn't seem too excited about the whole thing."

"Oh, by the way," Andy said. "I looked up in the dictionary what Sat could stand for. It usually is an abbreviation for Saturday, but can also stand for the planet Saturn. Then there was one more possibility — the Scholastic Aptitude Test. I asked Mom what that meant and she said it was a test that students who want to go to college often take. I think it helps colleges know whether to let the students come there or not."

"I can't believe it stands for Saturn," Jason offered. "And I doubt that our mysterious messenger is warning us that the Scholastic Aptitude Test is coming!" Both boys laughed.

"I agree," Andy replied. "For now, let's assume that Sat stands for Saturday."

Chapter Eleven

At supper, everyone seemed in a good mood. Andy looked around the table. He was glad God had given him this home to grow up in. How he loved his mom, dad, sister and brothers. Meal time was a happy time at the Nelson home.

Food was passed and Dad shared some of the things that happened at the mill that day. "John hired a new young man at the mill. His name is Pete."

"What's he like?" Mom asked. "Does he seem to be a hard worker?" All too often the new hires at the mill didn't work out. Dad said that no one seemed to want to work anymore. It was getting harder and harder to find someone who was willing to put in a full day's work.

"Well, I can't exactly say yet," Dad commented. "His job is to stack the newly-sawn boards as they come off the line. Alfred sorts the boards by grade. Some boards are just naturally a higher grade than others. Anyway, Pete's job is to stack the boards after Alfred grades them. Pete seemed to be working fine for a while. Then Alfred marked a board as a number one grade. Pete, however, put it in the number two grade stack. I just happened to walk by as this happened and called it to Pete's attention. 'Oh, Alfred must have missed seeing this discoloration,' Pete said confidently. 'That particular stain won't affect the grade,' I corrected him. Can you believe that? It was his first day on the job! Alfred's been marking lumber

The Mysterious Message

for years." Then looking at his children, Dad continued. "Children, remember to listen to those who have more experience in something. They're usually right. Not always. But usually!"

Ben listened to this story, then had much to say about playing in the pools of water in the yard. "Yes, I can testify that Ben indeed had fun in the water," Mom said. "His clothes and my floors are proof!"

"I have a letter I would like to read," Cathy announced after the conversation had died down temporarily. "It's from Julie, my pen pal in Colorado." In the Nelson household, anytime the children got a letter it was read at supper so everyone could enjoy it. Also, by sharing their mail in this way, Mom and Dad were able to keep abreast of the topics of correspondence that their children were encountering. Everyone kept eating but listened expectantly as Cathy read:

Greetings Dear Sister in Christ,

I hope things are going well for you in Tennessee . . . In Colorado, things are going, well, fantastic! I have news, Cathy, and I couldn't wait to write you. Jessica, that's my oldest sister as you know, is starting a courtship with a young man in a nearby town. His name is Matthew. Apparently, he has been having conversations with Mom and Dad for a while . . . Anyway, Jessica is very happy. Matthew seems to be a strong Christian. So far, the thing that has impressed me the most about him is his humbleness. I've never met a guy who . . . Write when you have time. And be sure and tell me about the warm, sunny weather I'm sure you're still having. ☺ We've already had several blizzards here! ☹ Maybe I should package up some snow and send it your way. Think your brothers would like that? If you'll just send some warm weather, maybe we can make a deal . . .

Love in Christ,
Julie

Before Cathy could comment on her letter, Jason said, "You need to write her and tell her that we've had snow, too! That will surprise her."

Cathy didn't respond to Jason's statement. Instead, she addressed Mom. "Isn't it wonderful about Jessica? I know she has been so patient as she has waited for the Lord to bring a young man into her life."

"Yes, that is a real answer to prayer," Mom smiled at her daughter. She was thinking that it would not be too many more years before Cathy was in the same situation. Thankfully, that was a matter that she and Timothy had committed to prayer for many years now.

"What's a courtship?" asked Ben, slowly. It was as though he had heard of it, but couldn't remember the details or exactly how it worked. "And why do you need to pray for one?"

Andy interjected, "A courtship, Ben, is where two people get married, but only after talking for a long time. You see, you need to talk to learn things. Talk a lot, I mean." Andy seemed to need help in explaining.

Jason tried to fill in more facts. "Well, it's kind of like that. Actually, two people can court and not get married. But the real thing that makes it a courtship is that they never, ever go on a date! We don't believe in dating, do we Dad?"

Dad smiled at his two oldest sons. "Well guys, there is truth in what both of you said. Biblical courtship, Ben, is where both a man and a woman pray and ask God to help them find a mate. Here's how it often happens. The young man, in addition to praying, asks his parents for advice. If he finds someone he thinks God is leading him to marry, he talks to his parents and the young lady's parents. Her parents then learn more about the young man and pray for God's will to be revealed. Then, if both sets of parents agree, the young lady is told of the young man's interests in courting her. If she is willing, as Jessica is, then the couple will spend time together, in the company of their parents, and family. They will talk a lot, like Andy said, learning about each other. But instead of just dating to have fun, they will be talking and learning about each other's character traits, Christian maturity, desires, and dreams. Everyone will continue to pray. If it is God's will, then the young man will ask the young lady to marry him. Does that make sense, Ben?"

Ben had listened to his dad's explanation, but had also maintained a great deal of attention on eating his chili. He looked up to his dad and nodded in agreement. When he finished swallowing and took a drink, he said, "It sounds like a lot of work to me! Does a man **have** to do it?"

Everyone laughed. "Yes, it is a lot of work, but it's time and effort well spent!" Mom said happily.

Dad agreed. "It certainly is a valuable use of your

time. To answer your question, no, a man doesn't have to use courtship in order to get married. But we know it is one method God can use and bless in a mighty way. We've seen it work wonderfully for a number of families. And we're committed to it for our children.

"Well, boys, talking about time spent," Dad addressed Jason and Andy. "Have you spent any time today thinking of four questions for the Case of the Missing Gas?"

Jason and Andy looked at each other. "Yes sir, we did," Jason said. "I'm not sure how good they are but we'll give them to you." Pulling out his spiral note-book, he read over the list of questions, trying to decide which he would ask first. Finally, he settled on one and said, "Dad, who has keys to the lock on the gate? I mean is it possible that someone in your mill who has a key, came in after hours, stole the gas, and then locked it back up?"

"That's a good question," Dad praised. "Actually, to the best of my knowledge only John and Alfred have keys. Alfred has a key because he returns sometimes to haul sawdust to his and neighboring farms for bedding. I wouldn't worry about Alfred though. He's as honest as the day is long."

"Well then, you may not like our next question," Jason continued slowly. "We were wondering . . . we're not accusing . . . we were wondering if . . . Dad, is it possible that Mr. Popper stole his own gas and tried to pretend that it was someone else?"

Dad looked thoughtfully at Jason. "Yes, that is always possible, son. Sin has a way of wanting to cover itself up. The Bible tells us that men will try to deceive us and fool us into believing they are good. Can you imagine what it will be like when a man stands before God, who knows all things, and that man realizes that his sin did not go unnoticed by the One who really counts?" Dad paused to let everyone realize the seriousness of unconfessed and 'hidden' sin. "There is no sin hidden from God. Just always remember that.

"Now," Dad continued, "since I already know the solution to the case I can tell you that in fact, John Popper did not steal his own gas."

"I'm glad he didn't," Ben added enthusiastically. "He's a nice man." Ben noticed that Cathy was smiling at him. Thinking, although incorrectly, that Cathy wasn't convinced of Mr. Popper's "niceness," Ben added, "He lets me play on his sawdust pile!"

"I, too, am glad that Mr. Popper didn't do it," Jason said. "Okay, our next question is this. Is it possible that someone has been coming in during the day, while the mill is running, and stealing gas a little at a time each day? You know how loud the mill is when it's running full steam. Maybe someone drove in and filled a tank and then left before anyone saw them?"

"Connie, these boys are good detectives," Dad said. "It's a good thing they are on our side!" Then addressing the partners of The Great Detective Agency he added, "That would make some sense. But how could they be sure that no one was going to see them? How could they know that someone wouldn't come to the office to make a phone call?"

"I don't know," Andy said. "But it sounds like this is a possible solution."

"Let's say it is a possible solution and see if you can come up with some other questions to flesh it out," Dad said, smiling at the boys.

"Andy, do you want to ask our last question?" Jason turned to his brother.

"Sure. Dad, is the solution to the case that the gas has reappeared?" Andy asked.

"What do you mean?" Dad questioned, leaning forward in his chair.

"I mean, is it possible that there was some mistake? That the measurement he took the other day was off? You know, maybe he didn't read the gauge right or something like that. In other words, is it possible that the gas never was missing?"

"Let's say that's a possible solution to the case also. Now, just like for your other idea, see if you can come up with some more questions or solutions as to how that could occur." Dad was obviously pleased with The Great Detective Agency.

"You know, I had a thought today while I was at work," Dad added. "Why don't you get Cathy involved in this case? What about it, Cathy? How would you like to add your brain to this great Brain Trust to solve the mystery?"

Cathy seemed hesitant. She looked at the boys. "I don't know, Dad. I'm not exactly a partner in their firm. They might not like having an older sister helping them out."

Jason looked at Andy. Both nodded. "We would like to have Cathy help. That is if she wants to and has time," Andy added.

After supper the boys went out to do their chores. True to their new strategy, Jason went by and looked at the bees to see if any new clues could be found. Everything looked just as it had earlier in the day. Then after doing their chores, the boys took a quick walk down the path in the woods. It was getting dark and neither boy had a desire to tarry long in the gathering twilight. No new clues presented themselves, which suggested that perhaps the visitor they were having was making his appearance sometime during the night or early morning. "I guess we'll learn more about that tomorrow," Jason said. "If we have some kind of new clue tomorrow morning, we'll know that he must be coming during the night sometime."

During family devotions, Dad read from James, chapter three. "I have a new set of verses that I want our family to memorize," Dad said. "I just read them. It's James 3:13-15."

Who is a wise man and endued with knowledge among you? let him show out of a good conversation his works with meekness of wisdom. But if ye have bitter envying and strife in your hearts, glory not, and lie not against the truth. This wisdom descendeth not from above, but is earthly, sensual, devilish.

The family spent the next several minutes repeating the first part of the passage over and over again. Then Dad began to explain what the passage meant. "True wisdom will reveal itself in a number of things," Dad taught. "These include a good life, righteous deeds, and meekness. The later verses I read reinforce this. They say that true wisdom is peaceable, gentle, full of mercy, and good fruits. People without true wisdom will display the opposite. These verses list a few fruits of false wisdom: bitterness, envy, and quarreling. There are several practical applications for all of us in these verses."

Closing his Bible, Dad continued. "First, we want to pray that God would help us seek true wisdom and cultivate that spirit in our hearts. Second, the verses suggest that we can learn about someone's spiritual condition by their fruits. If they display the good things we just mentioned, then they have the true wisdom which comes from God. If not, then they do not have the truth, and they are probably not followers of God. Let's pray that God would help us discern those with true wisdom, so we can learn from them."

Dad then reached for a glass of water that was on the table beside his chair. "Water," he said, taking a drink. "We all enjoy water, don't we? It's easy to go to the sink and get a tall, clean glass of water. Tonight let's remember to pray for our brothers and sisters in Christ in Bangladesh. Christians in Bangladesh are not allowed to drink from public wells. In fact, they aren't even allowed to touch the wells. So they must either walk long distances for water or drill their own well. Thankfully, the Voice of the Martyrs has been able to help many Christians dig wells behind their homes, and the water is shared with other Christians in their village. Let's pray that God would continue to meet their needs. And let's not forget to thank God for blessing us with a clean, easy-to-get supply of water!"

After prayers, there was the usual activity of the boys getting ready for bed. As Andy poured himself a drink of water, he thought of those in Bangladesh. *Wow, I've got it so easy*, he thought. *God's really been good to me.*

The Mysterious Message

Ben seemed to be thinking about water also. After filling his glass, he just let the water continue to run, while he watched it. After a minute, this irritated Jason. "Don't waste water, Ben! Mom," he called into the hall, "Ben's wasting water again."

Mom came and straightened things out. Before long, the three boys were in their beds, settling down for the night.

As Andy lay down in his soft, warm bed, he thought about the many cases and clues. *What was happening to those bees? Would they ever get any more clues or would they have to admit defeat and say they couldn't solve the mystery?* Then Andy had a new thought. *What if the Case of the Mysterious Message was somehow related to the missing bees? Was it possible that the person entering their property was doing something to the bees, in addition to leaving them clues? If so, the biggest question was 'why?' What was going to happen on Saturday? And would it happen on this Saturday or some future Saturday?* In some ways Andy could hardly wait for Saturday to arrive. In other ways, he sort of dreaded the day's coming. Who was the person leaving them clues? Again, Andy was reminded that Mom didn't seem the least bit worried about the Case of the Mysterious Message. It just didn't make sense to him.

Then, Andy's mind focused on the Case of the Missing Gas. Now that was one case in which the partners felt good. Although they hadn't solved it yet, Dad had suggested that they might be on the right track. But what was it that Dad thought Cathy needed to do to help The Great Detective Agency solve the case? As Andy drifted off to sleep, he continued thinking about these questions. The final question that popped into his head before going to sleep was this: *Wonder what we're having for breakfast?*

Chapter Twelve

W ell, guys," Cathy said at breakfast on Friday morning. "Do you want me to work with you on your Case of the Missing Gas today?"

"Sure," Andy said. "Maybe after we do our lessons, we will have some time to work on it. Does that sound okay, Mom?"

Mom nodded, then looked at Dad and smiled. *I wonder what that was all about*, thought Andy.

"Mom, would it be okay for us to see if there are any new clues about the bees or the mysterious messages?" Jason added. "Promise. We won't take a long time and we will work extra hard on our lessons when we return."

"If it won't take you more than fifteen minutes I suppose that will be okay," Mom assented.

After breakfast the boys went out to do their morning chores. The horses, cows, and goats were glad to see the boys, but seemed to be even happier to see the fresh water that they provided. After the chickens were fed and watered, the boys raced to see if any clues could be found.

At the bee hives, things looked to be about the same as they had been. Again, the boys could see skunk tracks on the soft ground near the hives.

Hurrying down the path in the woods, the boys were excited about what they might find. Jason said that he thought they wouldn't find anything. "Why would someone want to come out at night and leave clues?" he argued. "No, I think we'll find that this man is coming during the day sometime."

Andy was less sure. "Coming at night would be a lot safer. If he came during the day, he could never be sure if someone might see him."

They rounded a curve in the path before coming to where the initial clues were found. Both boys suddenly got very alert. They paused, combed the woods with their eyes, and listened intently. If someone was there right now, watching them, they wanted to be able to spot him.

Andy whispered, "Can't see or hear anything unusual. Can you?"

Jason didn't answer out loud. He just shook his head and pointed down the path, suggesting with his finger that they should continue walking.

Andy's heart was racing as they cautiously proceeded down the path. Suddenly he wanted to look back. He turned and looked past Jason, who was walking closely behind him. Jason looked at Andy as if to ask, "Why did you turn around? Did you hear anything?" However, Jason didn't actually say these words. Instead, he looked at Andy, then turned around to look for himself. Neither boy noticed anything out of the ordinary, and once again, began to walk.

They were getting closer to the place where they had found the clue yesterday. Again, Andy thought about turning around to look behind them. *That's silly*, he thought. *I looked a few minutes ago and didn't see anything. I don't really hear anything back there. I just have a strong desire to look back.* Trying to control himself, Andy didn't turn around and look. After a few steps, however, he couldn't resist any longer. He stopped, turned, looked beyond Jason, and kept looking.

This time, Jason turned around right away. He kept looking also. Nothing in the tree tops. Nothing in the path. There seemed to be nothing. He turned around and looked at his brother.

Andy, however, didn't turn back around and walk. His eyes kept tracking over and over the scene before him. Then, without saying anything, he looked into his brother's eyes. Extending his right arm, he pointed to the ground about five feet away.

Jason turned and followed his brother's pointing finger. Not seeing anything, he turned back to Andy. "I don't see anything," he whispered.

"There. See it right at the base of that tree? That old hickory tree next to the small pine sapling. Do you see it now?" Andy waited for his brother to find the item.

Finally, Jason blurted out "Yes!" and slowly moved toward the object on the ground.

After looking carefully around the woods to see if anyone was watching them, Andy and Jason stooped down and examined the item. It was a small tin can without a label. It could have been lying in the woods for a long time and have nothing to do with the Case of the Mysterious Message. That didn't seem likely, though. It wasn't rusty and it wasn't full of water or snow or leaves. No, it had been placed there, certainly since the last snow fall.

Andy picked it up carefully and looked inside. There was nothing there. He held it up to his nose and tried to see if it had any odor. Handing it to Jason, he asked, "What do you think?"

Jason sniffed the inside of the can, then said, "I can't be sure. But it sort of smells like peas to me. What do you think was in it?"

"I would have guessed the same thing," Andy replied. "It couldn't have been here long or the smell would be gone from the can."

Jason looked around some more for clues. Seeing none, he began to move the leaves that had been under the can. "Ha!" he shouted, holding up a plastic bag with a note inside. "This is really weird, Andy!"

The boys no longer cared if anyone was watching them or not. They began to talk out loud and examine this new clue more closely. "It's just an ordinary plastic bag like Mom uses for our sandwiches when we take trips or go on a picnic," Andy observed. "But Mom doesn't usually use them to hold letters!" he finished, laughing nervously.

"Well, here goes," Jason said, opening the bag and reaching inside for the note. It was a small piece of paper, about 3" x 3" with the following message, written in very small, cursive handwriting on both sides of the paper:

To see this can took some doing. Good job. You really are pretty good. Then to know to dig down into the leaves shows even more skill. Your Nelson Detective Agency has some good detectives. What was in the can? Did you guess? Well, you will be seeing the contents of that can again. In fact, you may actually consume some of it. Hope you're ready for it!

The Mysterious Message

It's probably light now, when you're reading this. It wasn't when I put the can here. You don't know me now. But you will soon. geb

"Wow!" Andy exclaimed. "We have a lot of clues in that letter. Too bad we can't work on it now. Remember, Mom said we only had fifteen minutes to check here. We better get back to the house."

The boys raced back to the house. It felt good to run because it used up some of the adrenaline their bodies had produced while looking for the clues. By the time they reached the house, they were breathing hard and had smiles on their faces. Andy took the can, the plastic bag and the letter and put them in The Great Detective Agency's office. "At least we have something to do later, partner," he commented.

Walking upstairs, they found Mom sitting at the kitchen table looking at an old photograph. "We're here, Mom," Jason said. "It didn't take us any longer than we thought. And thanks a bunch for letting us go! We found some more clues!"

Mom listened to their clues with a smile on her face. "That certainly does sound interesting, boys," she said. "I hope you can solve it before long."

"Mom, have we had peas recently?" Andy asked, wondering if he might know the answer to the case.

"No we haven't, Andy," Mom replied. "But if you want some, we could have some for supper. Does that sound good?"

That wasn't exactly the answer Andy had expected. "No thanks," he replied. "I mean, sure, we can have them if you want to, Mom. But don't have them just for me." Then noticing the picture again, he asked, "What are you looking at?"

"Oh, it's just an old picture of where I grew up in Illinois," she replied. "This is the newer barn that was built when I was a little girl," turning the picture around so that the boys could see it better. "My sister Amy, that's your Aunt Amy, found it in an old suitcase and sent it to me. I was just thinking about what it was like when I grew up."

"You say that barn was built new when you were little?" Jason asked. "It looks pretty old-fashioned to me."

Mom smiled. "I'm not exactly a young lady anymore, Jason. Of course, my dad did build the new barn with a lot of old-fashioned, interesting features. So it would look even older than it is."

"Hey, what's that?" Andy asked, pointing to an area beside the barn. The area he pointed out was grassy, yet had some deep dips. It looked like something had caved in at one time. "Was it a cellar or something?"

"Now, that's a good question," Mom began. Then, with a twinkle in her eyes, she said, "There used to be a railroad there." Even though both boys said "Neat!" at the same time in reply to this answer, Mom changed the subject. "It's past time for us to start lessons, guys. Run and get your notebooks and come back here for instructions."

Chapter Thirteen

Andy and Jason returned to the kitchen in a few minutes with notebooks and pencils. It had taken a while to find pencils. Those things seemed to always be disappearing. Of course, they also seemed to appear at the wrong places, like on the top of the refrigerator, in the washing machine, and on the floor, especially under the couch. In fact, Andy usually looked under the couch first if he couldn't find his pencil.

"Do you want me to work more on fractions?" Jason asked.

"Not this morning," Mom answered, with a big smile on her face. "This morning we are going to study history."

Both boys seemed disappointed, but tried not to let it show. "Yes ma'am," they said. "What do you want us to study?" Jason inquired.

Mom picked up the picture she had been studying earlier. She held it up for the boys to see closely. "I want you to study about this railroad," she began. "I want you to tell me how it got there, what it was used for, and why it is no longer there. Can you remember those three questions?" Then, assuming that they might forget one or more of them, she wrote the three questions in their notebooks.

"Well, aren't you going to teach us?" Andy asked, perplexed. "I would like to know about that railroad.

Do you not know the answers to these questions?"

Mom laughed. "Yes, of course I do. But don't you see? I'm going to let this be a sort of mystery for your agency. We can call it the Case of the Missing Railroad. I want you to look up the answers to my questions and then give me an oral report on what you find. If you get stuck or have questions about what to do next, just ask. But try to find it out on your own, okay? As a hint, I would suggest that you start by looking in our encyclopedias. Remember, I said it was a railroad. I said it was used for something. I also said it is no longer there. Any questions?"

"Why would the encyclopedia have something about the railroad at your farmhouse in Springfield, Illinois, Mom? It wasn't a famous railroad or anything like that," Jason said.

"I wouldn't be so sure about that," she smiled confidently. "You just might be surprised when you learn about this railroad. Any more questions?"

The boys looked at each other. "Not right now," Andy answered for both. "This is going to be fun!"

"Oh no, it can't be fun." Mom's eyes twinkled. "Remember that you don't really care for history."

"I'm not so sure about that now," replied Andy. "Let's go, Jason. I think we should look up the word 'railroad' first . . ." His voice trailed off as the duo walked toward the set of encyclopedias in the living room.

For quite a while, "Neat" and "Wow" and "Look at that" could be heard frequently coming from the living room. Ben raced over to see what his older brothers were finding. The boys found many exciting pictures of trains and the men who worked on them.

The Mysterious Message

In fact, they got so sidetracked looking at these pictures that, for a while, they forgot what their assignment was.

Mom walked over to where they were sitting after about thirty minutes and asked, "What kind of progress are you making?"

Jason and Andy looked up, sheepishly. "Not much, I'm afraid," Jason offered. "They have the neatest pictures in here of trains. But . . . we'll start reading about railroads now and see what we can find."

The boys then spent a good bit of time reading about railroads. They read carefully about how railroads help the public, what makes up a railroad, and the signals and safety devices used. Then they reached the section entitled "The History of Railroads." "Now we're getting somewhere," Andy said aloud.

In reading about railroad history, the boys were interested to learn that the first roads of rails could be traced back as far as the mid 1500's. "That's a lot older than Mom's farmhouse!" Andy laughed. "I doubt that is the answer we're supposed to find."

Jason agreed. They continued reading. They learned about the introduction of all-iron rails, an improvement over the wooden rails that came first. The steam engine and its impact on railroads fascinated the boys. When they learned that the name of an early locomotive was the *Tom Thumb*, both boys laughed. "That doesn't sound like a very powerful train to me!" Jason commented.

When they read that a horse had outrun the *Tom Thumb* in a famous race, Andy laughed, "With a name like that, it's no wonder."

The boys continued reading about the founding of new railroad companies and the laying of many miles of track. "This must be where it starts talking about the railroad on Mom's property," Jason said. They read even more carefully, looking for some clue which would point them to the railroad on Mom's farm. But none of the railroads were mentioned as specifically being near Springfield, Illinois.

When the boys started reading about the exciting gold rush of 1849 and the need to find a way to transport men and equipment to the booming California area, they were sure they had the answer to the Case of the Missing Railroad. Reading carefully, they learned that this railroad, called the Union Pacific, was finished in 1869 and that a golden spike was driven into the ground to complete it. "Wow!" exclaimed Andy. "Seems like a waste to use gold for a railroad spike!"

"I agree," Jason laughed. "Wouldn't it be neat to find that spike today? It's probably worth a lot of money now."

"I wonder if this is the railroad that went through Mom's farm?" Andy asked, getting back on the subject when he noticed that Mom was looking at them from the kitchen. "Where does it say it was located exactly?"

"Let's see," Jason said. "It went from Omaha, Nebraska to the San Francisco Bay in California. Let's get a map and see if that comes near Springfield, Illinois. I don't think it does, though."

Sure enough, looking at a map only confirmed Jason's fears. "Well, that was sure a pretty important

The Mysterious Message

railroad. It joined the Atlantic and the Pacific oceans with a railroad and made it so that people could travel across the country in just a few days. But it can't be the one we need to find out about."

"Let's keep reading and see what else we can find," Andy suggested. "Maybe there are some more important railroads mentioned." The boys continued reading about the history of railroads and their rise in importance. Then they read about the leading railroad companies in the United States, how railroads have been regulated by the government, and finished by learning about jobs in railroading.

"It would be neat to be an engineer," Jason said.

"I think I would rather be a brakeman," Andy replied. "They get to hang off the train while it's moving."

They finished the long article on railroads just as Mom was calling them to eat lunch. "Having any success, boys?" Mom asked.

The boys related their search and what they had found. "Well, you didn't learn about the railroad on our property," she said. "But you did learn some interesting things about railroads."

During lunch, Andy questioned, "What should we do now? I mean, there wasn't anything about a railroad on your property, Mom. Where should we look?"

Cathy offered a suggestion. "Why not look at the end of the article on railroads and see what other related articles they suggest? Also, you may want to try looking at the research guide that came with the encyclopedias. You can save a lot of time by looking at indexes, I've found."

"Will you help us?" asked Jason. Then looking at Mom, he added, "Is that okay, Mom, for her to help us?"

Mom smiled. Part of the joy of homeschooling was watching brothers and sisters helping each other learn. "I think that would be a great idea, Jason. Maybe you three can also work on the Case of the Missing Gas. I'll let those be your lesson assignments for this afternoon."

After lunch, Mom again gave the boys permission to check on clues after doing their chores. There were no new clues either at the bee hives or on the trail in the woods. When they returned, Cathy was waiting in the kitchen. "Are you ready for me to work with you?"

"I think so," Andy answered for the pair. "What should we work on first?"

"Since we were working on the railroad issue right before lunch, I think it would make sense to keep working on that," Jason decided. So they did.

"Let's get the encyclopedia out again and look at the end of the article on railroads," Cathy suggested. "See," she pointed out, "there are about fifty related articles that we could look up."

Both boys groaned. "That will take us forever," worried Andy. "It took us about all morning just to read and study the one article on railroads."

Cathy laughed. "We don't have to read each one. We can usually get some idea of whether or not they would be helpful just from their title. For example, sixteen of these articles are just biographies. Biographies tell the life story of someone. So in this case, the biographies tell the life story of some important men

The Mysterious Message

who started railroads or did research about railroads."

Both boys were listening carefully. "For instance, one biography is about the life of Peter Cooper," Cathy said.

"I know who that is!" remembered Jason. "He is the man who built and raced the *Tom Thumb*. He lost, too!"

"Okay," said Cathy. "We know that his biography will probably give us lots more information about the Tom Thumb. Is that something that will help us solve the Case of the Missing Railroad?"

"I don't think so," Jason admitted. "We already know that doesn't have anything to do with it."

"So you see," Cathy concluded, "we can rule out that article. We don't have to try that one because it won't really help us. In fact, seeing this list of biographies, it doesn't seem as though any of them will help us. So, let's look at the list of other related articles. One is on 'brakes.' Would that help us?"

"It would probably be real interesting!" Andy offered hopefully. Jason laughed. "But I guess it wouldn't really help us."

"Let's look at some other related article titles," Cathy continued. "Would 'Tom Thumb' or 'Locomotive' or 'Japan' or 'Caboose' help us?"

Both boys shook their heads. "Any article titles that we aren't sure about, we can look up. But we don't have to read the whole article. We can just skim them to see if they mention, in this case, anything about Springfield, Illinois," Cathy instructed.

Cathy helped the boys look up "Gadsden Purchase" which didn't prove helpful. After looking up several related articles, she admitted that none of them were going to help the boys solve their mystery.

"Didn't we just waste some time?" Jason asked.

"Not really," Cathy replied. "At least now we know what things are not going to help us. Of course, we need to keep looking until we find something that might help us. Let's look up railroads in the research guide and master index which came with the encyclopedias."

When she pulled out that volume, Jason commented, "I've never used that before. Does it have any good pictures in it?" As Cathy thumbed through the pages, Jason saw the answer to his question. "Hey, there's not one single picture in that whole big book!"

Cathy laughed. "That's right. It's not supposed to have pictures to keep you interested. It's just a list of articles, by subject, so you can look them up. The pictures are with the article, not with the index." Finding the entry for railroad, she read some of the topics out loud. "Well, we could look up subjects like Coal, Industrial Revolution, Transportation, or Western Movement. See, each of those articles will mention railroad in some way. By using this index, you find every mention of railroad in all twenty-one volumes of this encyclopedia set. That would surely be quicker than turning every page of every volume."

The boys agreed with her. As they studied the subjects listed, however, they didn't feel that any would help them learn more about a railroad in Springfield, Illinois. Looking up Illinois in the encyclopedia didn't really help either.

"Now what do we do?" questioned Andy. "Should we go ask Mom for some hint?"

The Mysterious Message

Cathy wanted to search in several other places first. She and the boys tried some of their textbooks on American history, geography, and world history. In each of these books, they looked up the subject 'railroad' in the index in the back to see if anything was mentioned that might solve the Case of the Missing Railroad. Cathy then found the dictionary and looked under 'railroad.' It had several definitions, but none that helped them solve their mystery. "Well, guys, I'm not sure where to look now."

"What about that great big dictionary that we have?" asked Andy. "You know, Jason, that one we used to hold down the paper when we were gluing up a paper kite last spring."

"Oh, you must mean the unabridged dictionary," said Cathy. "Sure, we can try it, too." Finding the word 'railroad' she handed the book to the boys. It was so heavy that it sort of hurt Andy's lap to have it there.

Most definitions were like the ones they had already read. Then Jason read some of the other information provided at the end of the definitions. "The underground railroad, prior to 1861, was a system in the United States set up by certain opponents of slavery to help fugitive slaves from the South escape to free States and Canada.' Now that sounds interesting!"

Cathy stood up and started to walk out of the room. "Where are you going?" asked Andy.

"I think you guys may have stumbled onto something helpful," she responded. "I'll let you work on that a while, then later we can discuss the Case of the Missing Gas. Okay?"

"Sure," Jason and Andy agreed. After Cathy left, Jason said to Andy, "Well, from the way Cathy acted, this underground railroad must be important to solving the Case of the Missing Railroad."

"Yes, it must be. What should we do now?" asked Andy.

"Let's look up underground railroad," answered Jason. They did and learned all about how slaves were rescued and transported to safety through this thing called the underground railroad. "It wasn't really a railroad or underground. It was called that because it was a fast, secret way for slaves to escape," commented Jason after reading a few lines in the encyclopedia. "It says that Ohio and Pennsylvania were the most active states for this, but by the time the Civil War broke out, every northern state was helping out. I guess that includes Illinois, too."

"Wow, look at this," Andy said, pointing to a section in the book. "It says that over 50,000 slaves escaped in this way. That's a lot of people."

"Yes, and this lady, Harriet Tubman, who was once a slave herself, kept going back to the South and helping more slaves escape. She helped over 300 slaves escape! I'd say she was pretty brave! Slave owners even offered a huge reward to anyone who could capture her."

"Let's go ask Mom if the railroad at her farm was a part of the underground railroad," Andy said.

"That's right," Mom answered when asked by the boys. "My great-great-grandparents had an area under their barn where they hid runaway slaves during the day. Then at night, the slaves would leave our farm and most would make their way up to Chicago. That

The Mysterious Message

would take many days and be very dangerous. But there were others farms and houses like ours where they could hide, rest, and get food. When the slaves got to Chicago, they would get on a boat and travel to Canada. In Canada they were finally free."

"So you had a tunnel in your farm?" Ben asked. He had been listening to this conversation. "A tunnel that went all the way to Chicago?"

Mom smiled. "No, honey. We had a dug-out place under the floor boards of our barn where escaped slaves would hide. Then when they were ready to move further north, toward their freedom, they would come out of their hiding place at night and walk toward Chicago. Sometimes people would even hide the slaves in their wagons. In that way, the slaves wouldn't have to do so much walking. Anyway, there were people all over the country side that would help the runaway slaves. You could think of all of those helping people and all of those hiding places as the 'underground railroad.' Even though it was called the underground railroad, it wasn't really a train or one single tunnel that the slaves used. Does that make sense?"

"Yes ma'am," Ben responded. "I think those people were really nice to help the runaway slaves."

"The Case of the Missing Railroad is solved!" Andy said. Both boys were happy not only to solve the mystery, but also to learn something so interesting.

"History isn't so boring, is it?" asked Mom.

"No!" both boys agreed.

"That was really fun," added Jason. "Now, it's time to tackle the Case of the Missing Gas. Have you seen Cathy?"

Chapter Fourteen

Before long Cathy and the two boys were in the living room discussing the case. Cathy was ironing while she talked. "Dad seemed to hint that two of your questions last night might be on the right track," she said. Picking up the next shirt, she smoothed it out over the ironing board while the boys watched. There was something mesmerizing about watching someone else iron clothes. "First, let's think about your suggestion that someone might be stealing the gas during the daytime while everyone in the mill is busy. For that to happen what would have to occur?"

"I don't know what you mean," Andy said.

"Just this. Let's assume for the moment that someone **is** stealing gas during the day. Okay. Obviously that means that no one could see them. Right? Well, what else would have to be true?"

"I guess they would also have to have a way to pump the gas," Jason said. "Is that what you mean?"

"Exactly," said Cathy. "What else?"

"They would have to have something to put the gas into," volunteered Andy, beginning to understand what Cathy was trying to do. "They would also probably want to have some excuse ready if someone caught them doing it. You know, something like, 'John told me to fill this tank and deliver it to the other side of the mill.'"

"That's good," Cathy praised. "Anything else?"

The Mysterious Message

The boys thought and thought but couldn't come up with anything else. "Okay, let's see how realistic those things are. First, is it really possible that no one would see them while they pumped? Is the tank located somewhere that no one who is working at the mill would be able to see it?"

"That's a great question," Jason noted. "I think we should ask Dad that tonight!" Andy agreed with him.

"How fast could someone get the gas out of the tank?" Cathy asked.

"I think it would come out real fast," Andy said.

"I'm not sure," replied Jason. "I mean, if you cut a hole in the side of the tank, sure it would come out fast. But they must have some way to slow the gas from coming out too fast. Probably some kind of switch or controller. You know, Andy, I think that's another question to ask Dad."

"What was the other thing we thought of?" Looking at his list in his spiral notebook, he answered his own question. "Oh, yeah. What would they pump it into?" He looked at Cathy. "Do you think they could have a tank in the back of their truck or inside their van that would hold the gas?"

"I think so," Cathy said. "Having something to put it into shouldn't be a problem. But I just thought of something else. In order for someone to pump gas out of the tank, they need a hose. Does the mill always keep a hose hooked up to the tank? Or do they keep the hose inside somewhere, and just hook it up when they need to pump some out? I really don't know. Of course, if the fittings are pretty standard, it may be easy for the thief to bring in his own hose."

"I guess we better ask Dad that question also," Jason said, writing it in his notebook. "That's three questions already, and we haven't even talked about the other possible solution to the case yet."

"You mean that the gas has reappeared or that it never disappeared in the first place?" Cathy asked. Jason nodded. "That's going to be tougher to figure out, it seems to me. We need to figure out how it could have reappeared. Or how it had never disappeared in the first place, but under conditions that made Mr. Popper **think** that it had disappeared."

"Well, what kinds of questions would help us figure out if that is a possibility?" Andy inquired. He really understood now Cathy's method of evaluating the possible solutions.

"Maybe we should ask a very simple question: Did Mr. Popper make some kind of error as he measured the amount of gas in the tank?" said Jason. "What do you think, Andy?"

"I think that is a very good question to ask. It looks like we have our four questions. I can't wait for Dad to come home so we can ask them."

Cathy hung up the shirt she was ironing and reached for a wrinkled one. "It will be interesting," she agreed.

"Thanks for your help, Cathy," Jason said.

"Yes, thanks," Andy echoed. "I think we have some good questions because of your help."

After checking in with Mom to see if she had anything they needed to do, they went outside to check for new clues. Nothing new presented itself either at the bee hives or in the woods.

That night at supper, the boys had many things to

The Mysterious Message

tell their dad. The Case of the Missing Railroad was explained with so much enthusiasm that Mom had to calm the boys down a bit for fear that they might choke on their food. The latest clues of the Case of the Mysterious Message were revealed, which generated some interesting facial expressions from Dad. It was hard to tell, though, if he was worried, just interested, or amused.

"What about the Case of the Missing Bees?" Dad asked. "How's that going? I sure do like our good honey and would hate to see it disappear on us."

Andy sort of squirmed in his seat. "We haven't found out anything new, Dad. Do you have any ideas that might help us?"

"Not really," Dad admitted. After a few seconds, he added, "Have you looked it up in any books?"

"Yes sir," Andy said. "We looked up the tracks in a book and found out they were made by skunks."

"Yes, but have you tried to find out if skunks steal honey, or anything like that?" Dad queried.

The boys had to admit that they hadn't considered doing that. "We'll do that tomorrow," Jason said.

"While you're at it, you may want to look in as many sources as you can find, to see if you get any new ideas," Mom offered. "Your success today with the Underground Railroad has given you some better skills at doing that kind of research."

"That's a really good idea!" Andy said. "We could look up 'bees', 'skunks' and things like that in the research guide of the encyclopedia."

"Yes, and we could look at other books we might have with information about bees or animals," Jason added. "We'll get on it tomorrow morning."

97

Cathy smiled as she realized that she had really helped her brothers develop their research skills today. She was willing to answer any questions they might have tomorrow. In fact, the more she thought about the Case of the Missing Bees, the more she wondered why she hadn't done more research herself before going to The Great Detective Agency for help. After supper, if she had time, she was going to do a little research on her own.

"Now, what about the Case of the Missing Gas?" Dad asked. "Do you have your questions ready for me?"

"Yes sir," Jason said. "Cathy really helped us a lot. Andy, why don't you ask the first question?"

"Okay. Dad, is the big tank at your mill located somewhere so that it is hidden from people while they are working? I mean, let's say that everyone is busy at their job at the mill. Is there anyone who has a good view of the tank from where they usually sit or stand?"

"That's a good question," Dad said. "Actually, the tank is located at the back side of the mill. A wall shields the tank pretty well from being seen by anyone inside."

Andy and Jason looked at each other with satisfied glances. Dad wasn't through talking, though. "Of course," he continued, "there are people who don't have one specific place to stand or sit all the time. Like me. I drive my fork lift all over the mill site all day long. Several other men do the same thing. The tank is not shielded from my sight if I'm driving around the outside of the building. I guess there are four or five of us who always seem to be moving around the mill or outside the mill. And it would be hard for someone to predict where I'm going to be anytime, either, as far as that goes."

The boys' satisfied facial expressions had changed to something more resembling humbleness. Jason was ready to offer his next question. "Dad, is there a hose on the tank that stays there? I mean, if you wanted to pump some gas out, would you have to go and find a hose to use, or is there always one hooked up to the gas tank?"

"Yes, there is a hose at one end of the tank that is always connected," Dad answered. "We use it to fill our fork lifts."

"How long does it take to pump the gas?" Andy questioned. "Does it take a long time, or can someone pump it pretty quickly?"

"You sure do have some good questions," praised Dad. "Let's see, I think ours is set to release about fifteen gallons a minute."

"That's seems awfully fast!" Andy exclaimed. "How long would it take to fill a good sized tank, then?" He quickly added, "That's not considered another question, is it?"

"No, we'll count it as being part of your third question. The pump can fill a 500-gallon tank in a little over thirty minutes. Maybe that gives you some idea." Dad buttered a roll. "You have one more question?"

"Yes sir," Jason said. "Did Mr. Popper make some kind of error as he measured the amount of gas in the tank?"

Dad thought about that question for a few minutes before answering. Because of Dad's silence, the room got quiet. The atmosphere seemed more like what you would find in a library than what you would find in an average family, eating supper. "That is a hard question to answer. I think I'm going to say that the answer is both 'yes' and 'no'."

The boys looked at each other with confused, but excited faces.

"What kind of error did he make?" asked Jason, excitedly.

"Ah, that's a question, and you've already used up your four for tonight!" Dad laughed. "I guess we'll have to wait for tomorrow night for that one."

After supper, the boys did their evening chores, then looked for new clues at the bee hives and in the woods. Not finding any, they walked back toward home, talking mostly about the Case of the Missing Gas as they went along. Suddenly, Jason stated, "Hey, we never did study that clue we got this morning in the woods. It's still on the desk in our office! We've been so busy that I forgot all about it. Now it's so late that we will have to wait until tomorrow to do much with it."

"That's okay," said Andy. "Chances are that we will have another clue to add to it tomorrow morning." Looking back down the darkening trail behind him, Andy said rather loudly, "Who are you? What are you up to?" Hearing no reply, and certainly not expecting to, the boys finished their walk home. It had been a very busy day, and Andy, especially, was tired.

At devotions on Friday night, the family worked more on their new Bible verse. Most everyone had memorized the first two sentences in the passage. It was fun with Mom and Dad also trying to learn the verses. This taught the children that memorizing Bible verses were important for people of all ages, even those who had been Christians for many years.

Dad chose the Old Testament story of Elisha and the axe head found in II Kings 6 for the evening Bible reading. "In the story I'm about to read, one of the servants lost a borrowed axe head as he was cutting down a tree," he explained before reading the passage. "It was made out of iron and sank down into the water. What would you do if that happened to you?"

"I'd run and tell on myself," Ben announced, honestly.

Andy said, "I think I'd swim around and try to find it with my toes."

"You might end up cutting your toes on the sharp axe!" Ben proclaimed.

"How about using a big magnet tied to a string?" Jason wondered.

"I think I would tell Elisha and see what he could do to help," Cathy offered next.

"Humph," Dad grunted, with eyes twinkling. "Seems like at least one person is familiar with the passage!" After reading the scripture, Dad answered his own question.

"The servant did run and tell Elisha about the problem. Elisha asked the servant to show him where the axe head had disappeared in the water. After tossing a stick into the water, the iron axe head swam."

"Now that's what I call a miracle!" Jason exclaimed.

"That's right," Dad said.

"I wish God would do that kind of thing today," Ben said sadly. "It would be fun to see."

"Actually, God still does miracles today," Dad corrected his son. "People are completely healed from diseases that doctors say are totally incurable. You all remember how we prayed for Mr. Mathers who had liver cancer so badly that the doctors gave him only a week to live."

"Yes," Andy remembered. "And now he is totally well. Doctors can't find anything wrong at all with his liver!"

"That's right. And God does other kinds of miracles also," Dad added. "From the Voice of the Martyrs newsletters we receive, we have read of many miracles that God has performed. Tonight as we pray, let's ask God to perform a miracle in the war-torn nations of Africa. Let's pray that the bloodshed and violence would end and that Africans would come to a saving knowledge of Jesus Christ. We have seen what God did in the former USSR. Nothing is too hard for Him."

After prayers and hugs, the boys trudged up the stairs. Andy was grateful that it was his bedtime. He couldn't remember when he had been so tired. Looking over at Jason and Ben, he said, "Good night." Soon he was sound asleep.

Chapter Fifteen

Saturday started off as a beautiful, warm morning. Could it really have snowed just a few days ago? The morning air was filled with the sound of birds singing. Even with the windows closed, Andy could hear the birds clearly. "Sounds like springtime to me," Andy said, stretching as he lay in bed.

"I like to hear the birds singing so much," Ben agreed, trying to make his bed. The sheet was hanging so far down on one side of the bed that it was touching the floor. Ben continued to struggle with the blanket, trying to arrange it into some semblance of order. "Do you think there will be any puddles left?"

"I doubt it," Jason replied. He was almost finished dressing and was putting away his pajamas. Looking out the window, he continued, "I don't see any puddles from here. Of course, there could be some out near the barn or woods."

Turning to Andy, Jason prodded, "You better get out of bed, Andy, before I go out and solve all of our mysteries myself! We've got a big day ahead of us. And it's Saturday, too! Dad's home all day long."

"Yeah!" Ben cheered enthusiastically. "Maybe he'll do something fun with us!"

"Maybe," echoed Andy. "The Great Detective Agency will be busy today. We need to check on new clues for the Case of the Missing Bees and the Case of the Mysterious Message, and then try to solve the

Case of the Missing Gas." He turned to Jason. "I just feel like this is going to be a real good day for our agency, partner."

"Me too," Jason agreed. Both boys were still excited about solving the Case of the Missing Railroad yesterday. "What should we do first?"

"Eat breakfast!" Ben answered, walking out the door and heading toward the kitchen.

Andy laughed. The more he thought about it, the more he agreed. "What does that smell like?" he wondered aloud, sniffing the air carefully.

"I've already been trying to figure it out. Smells like cinnamon and raisins cooking. Could be muffins, or a coffee cake, I guess." Just talking about it made Jason hurry and finish making his bed. "Better hurry, Andy. Smells like whatever it is should be about ready!"

Andy was already hurrying. "I'm coming. Just need to put away these clothes." With a quick toss of the clothes into the drawer, Andy raced out the door behind his brother.

"It's coffee cake!" announced Ben as the boys entered the kitchen. "And we have grape juice, milk, and eggs to go with it."

"Mom, how soon will we eat?" Jason asked.

"Soon. Really soon, guys," Mom answered, smiling at her crew of boys, who were gazing toward the stove with sweet anticipation.

Cathy, who was cooking the eggs, smiled also. "Whenever you guys need my help today, you just let me know," she said. "Mom and I are going to run to town this morning, but we should be back by 10:30 or 11:00."

The Mysterious Message

"Would you boys like to come?" Mom asked. "I'm going to be going by the hardware store."

"Yes ma'am," Ben responded quickly. "I love the hardware store."

Andy and Jason looked at each other. It was a hard decision. As much as they loved to go to the hardware store, they also wanted to work on their mysteries. Finally, Jason said, "I think I would like to stay home this morning, Mom."

"Me too," Andy agreed. "We have a lot of detective work to do."

Dad walked into the kitchen, humming the hymn *When We All Get to Heaven*. "Good morning, folks," he said cheerfully. "What a beautiful morning the Lord has made. Even the horses seemed in especially good spirits this morning." He walked over and rubbed Cathy's back. "What are you cooking there, young lady?"

"Scrambled eggs," Cathy laughed. It was obvious what she was cooking. This was just Dad's way of asking 'How soon will they be ready?' So Cathy added, "And they will be ready very soon."

Before long, everyone was sitting down to eat. The conversation was not unlike that found in many homes on a Saturday morning. Mom asked Dad if he needed anything from town. When Dad mentioned that he needed some rope, it caused Cathy to suddenly remember that she needed a few yards of piping for a new sewing project she planned to start next week. These items were added to their list.

"I suppose you boys are going to be busy this morning?" Dad asked.

"Well, we did have some things we had planned on

doing," Andy answered. "But if you need us for anything we would be happy to help." The boys always enjoyed working with Dad.

"We need to do a little cleaning in the barn," Dad said. "I noticed that it's getting pretty junky again. It shouldn't take us more than an hour or two." He put another piece of coffee cake on Ben's plate before continuing. "But you boys can have about an hour after breakfast to do whatever you like. I have some paperwork to finish, and I can do that as easily this morning as anytime. In fact, it would be nice to get it in today's mail."

"Thanks," Jason said. "We'll keep checking with you and see when you're ready for us."

After breakfast the boys headed out to do their chores. As they walked by the bee hives, Andy spoke. "We really need to take Dad's advice and look up bees in our books. Maybe the solution to our mystery is there just waiting for us!"

"Let's tackle that as soon as we get back in the house," Jason agreed.

The boys did their barn chores. Leaving the barn, Jason asked, "Should we maybe see if there's another clue in the woods before we go in?"

Andy thought about it a minute. "Sure, why not? I'm pretty curious to see if there's anything out there."

The boys walked down the trail looking carefully. They looked up in trees and behind rocks. "What's that?" asked Jason, quickly stopping in the path. When Andy apparently couldn't see anything, Jason added, "Over there, hanging in that tree?"

"I don't know," Andy said. "Looks like some kind of a handle or something. Let's go get it."

The Mysterious Message

The boys left the path and walked into the woods about twenty feet. The closer they got to the mysterious object, however, the less mysterious it seemed. "It's just a branch that fell off the tree," Jason laughed. "But from back there it looked just like a broom handle."

"I know," Andy agreed. "At first, I thought someone had taken Mom's broom and torn off the bristles." Now that the boys were right next to the branch, they almost felt silly that they had even considered it a clue. Jason grabbed the branch and decided to use it as a walking stick. Turning around, they went back to the path.

Passing the place where the first clue was found, the boys saw nothing out of the ordinary. No one had rebuilt the pile of rocks that Jason had dismantled while searching for additional clues a few days ago. Still, it seemed like there should be some new clue in the area. Not seeing anything, though, the boys had no choice but to continue walking.

"Maybe he didn't come last night," Andy offered.

Jason didn't respond. The boys went around another bend in the path.

"It seems like we should have seen something by now," Jason commented. "We're almost to where we found the last clue." Still, the boys didn't see anything out of the ordinary. Before long they had walked to the edge of their property.

"Well, I guess he didn't come last night," Jason finally admitted. "Let's head back home and work on the clues we have."

"Yes," Andy said. "Maybe we'll see something on the way home that we missed."

Chapter Sixteen

But the boys found no new clues that Saturday morning. They speculated on what that meant. "Maybe he left something, but we didn't find it because he hid it too hard," Jason said.

"That is really possible," Andy agreed. "The clues do seem to be getting harder to find. What should we do now?"

"We can't really work on the Case of the Missing Gas until Cathy gets home. And Dad won't need us for a while. Why don't we work on the Case of the Missing Bees?"

The boys walked down to their basement office. "Let's review the clues we have so far," Jason said.

"There aren't very many," Andy reminded his partner. "We don't think it is a swarm, or disease, or ants. We found tracks of a skunk or skunks around the hives, but that is about it."

"Let's do what Dad suggested," Jason said. "Let's go and look up skunks in our books and see what they say. Who knows, maybe they like to eat bees!" Both boys laughed.

Reaching for the encyclopedia, Jason looked up 'skunk.' Actually, that took a little time. Not because he didn't know how to spell skunk. It took time because the boys were so interested in the pictures and articles they saw as they flipped to the word 'skunk.' They marveled and exclaimed over pictures of sail-

The Mysterious Message

boats, the Saint Lawrence Seaway, the rugged Highlands of Scotland, the Seven Wonders of the Ancient World, univalve and bivalve shells, and all the many different kinds of ships. In fact, they spent close to five minutes studying the clipper ship *Flying Cloud*.

Reluctantly, for it was hard to flip past the pictures of ships, they turned to 'skunk.' Jason read out loud the information provided.

"Wow Andy, imagine that! A skunk can squirt its smelly fluid up to ten feet with good aim!" Jason exclaimed. "We'd better not mess around with any skunks."

Reading further, the boys learned that skunks are active at night and usually sleep during the day. Skunks sleep through a lot of the winter months, although they don't really hibernate. "Now it tells about what they eat," Jason said. "Skunks eat insects, rats, mice, and other small animals. They also eat eggs. Except for the eggs, I wouldn't want to be a skunk!"

"I agree!" Andy said. "Does it say anything about bees?"

Jason read ahead in the book silently. "No, it doesn't. It talks some about their fur being valuable. Can you imagine Mom wearing a skunk coat?"

Andy and Jason laughed so hard that it was difficult for them to settle back down. Finally, Andy looked at the encyclopedia. "The related articles in the encyclopedia include animal, fur, pet, and polecat. It doesn't sound like any of those would help us." Looking at the encyclopedia's main index didn't provide any new clues either.

"Let's look at some of our books on animals and

see what they say," Jason suggested. The boys opened a small book on mammals. They were surprised by some of the new information they learned. "I thought the encyclopedia would tell us everything about skunks, but listen to this," Andy said. "Skunks give a clear warning before they squirt. They often stamp their front feet, hiss, and even raise their hair! I didn't know that."

"Yes, and it says that their babies are born blind. That's too bad."

"Sure, but they grow quickly, it says," replied Andy. "This book also says that they eat mice, rats, all kinds of insects, and adds the fact that they eat chipmunks, too."

Jason started thumbing through a larger, more complete book on North American mammals. Again, it was hard for him to keep his mind on the subject at hand. He kept stopping to look at the pictures of shrews, bats, voles, and beavers. Finally, he got to the page with pictures of skunks. "Hey, look at this!" he said loudly. Jason pulled a small piece of paper from the book. It had been stuck deep inside the book on the page with the picture of the skunk. The note read:

> Good work. You're on the right track. Don't give up!

"I wonder who put that in there!" Jason exclaimed.

Andy looked at the note carefully. "It looks like Mom's writing. Or maybe it's Cathy's writing. Well, whoever put it in there must know what we're doing and why. I wonder when it was put in?"

The Mysterious Message

"I don't know," Jason said. At the bottom of each picture in the book was a page number. That number indicated where, in the back of the book, an interested reader could learn more about the animal. "Page 653," Jason read out loud. "Let's see what that tells us about skunks that we don't already know." Turning to the back of the book, Jason shouted again, "Here's another note!" This note was in the same handwriting:

Great! You're not just looking at the pictures. Keep it up. You'll find the answers to your questions yet!

"This is exciting," Andy said. "What does it say about skunks?"

Jason read quickly. Then he laughed out loud. "Nothing much new."

"Then why did you laugh?"

"Just like the other book, it says that when a skunk is threatened it stomps the ground, and raises its tail hairs. But it also says that it will chatter its teeth. Can't you just see a skunk doing all of those things? If you don't get the message, then watch out! The skunk will twist around backward, raise its tail straight up and spray away!" Both boys laughed.

Jason was about to close the book when he noticed something. "Say Andy! This book says that skunks eat grasshoppers, crickets, worms, butterflies, wasps, and **bees!**"

"That's it!" Andy shouted. "I think we've solved the mystery. Sure, it must be skunks that are eating the bees!" Andy was very excited.

"You're right," Jason agreed. "But how can it get the bees out of the hives? I would think they are better protected in their hives, than say, some bees in an old tree or a rotten wall. Does it just stand there with its mouth open, hoping that a bee will fly into it?"

Andy laughed at the ridiculous scene Jason had sketched. "That's a good question. How could we find that out?"

The two investigators of The Great Detective Agency pondered this problem for a few minutes. "Why don't we look in some of the books we have about beekeeping? Maybe they have something that would help us out!"

Andy ran and got the two books that Cathy and Mom always used for finding information about how to care for their bees. At first, he just flipped through the pages trying to find a picture of a skunk. Then he remembered the index in the back of the book. Turning there quickly, he looked at the entries that began with the letter s: . . . section frames, section honey, section supers, shipping case, . . . skunks! His heart was pounding as he turned to page 213. When he finally found the page, he shouted again. There was another slip of paper, which read:

> Way to go! I think you've found the solution to the Case of the Missing Bees!

Reading the information in the book, the boys learned that skunks love to eat bees. "It says that the population will fall but without any known reason for the fall," Andy summarized. "Also, the remaining bees

The Mysterious Message

will become quite angry."

"You can say that again," Jason agreed, thinking of the many stings he encountered on Monday. "But how do they get the bees out of the hives?"

Reading further in the section, Andy began to smile. "Those silly skunks come around at night. They start scratching at the front of the hives, and wait for the bees to come out and investigate. Sometimes, they will bang on the sides of the hive to get the bees angry and make them come out. As soon as the bees come buzzing out, 'our friend' the skunk snaps them up!"

"It's solved!" Jason said. "The Case of the Missing Bees is really and truly solved."

"Hey, listen to this," Andy continued. "It says to solve this problem all we have to do is raise the hives two feet off the ground. Skunks will leave them alone if we will do that. This says that skunks would have to stand on their hind legs if the hives are two feet off the ground. Know why that's a problem?"

"No, why?" Jason asked.

"Because the bees will sting the skunk's soft underbelly," Andy finished. "And we can imagine how much fun that would be! I imagine the skunks hang around just about as long as we did when we started getting stung. Not long!"

After putting all of the books away, the boys ran to tell Dad what they had learned. They had to catch their breath a second before talking, however.

Dad was genuinely impressed. "I'm glad you guys aren't afraid to look in books for answers."

"Now that we know how to use books better, I guess we'll use them more often," Jason said.

"What I don't understand is who put those notes in the books for you to find. If it was Cathy, then why did she get The Great Detective Agency involved in the first place? Why not just solve the problem herself?" Dad wondered. "It would have saved some bees from attacks these last few nights."

"We don't understand that either," Jason said. "When she gets home, we're going to ask her."

"Are you boys ready to work in the barn now?" Dad asked, smiling at his great helpers.

"Yes sir," came the reply. Their energy level was high and their bodies were aching for some kind of physical exercise to work it off.

As they worked, Dad talked to them about the Case of the Missing Gas. "Have you started working on your questions for tonight?"

"Not yet," Andy said. "We haven't had time."

"Besides, Cathy won't be home for a while," Jason added. "She's going to help us."

"That would probably be a good idea," Dad agreed. Before long, the job of straightening up the barn was finished.

"Thanks for your help, guys. I think I'll split some firewood. You can take a break and do whatever you want. Later, we will all work stacking the wood."

Jason and Andy walked out of the barn into the warm midmorning light. "What should we do now?" Andy asked.

Chapter Seventeen

Why don't we go back down the trail again and see if there are any new clues?" Jason suggested.

"I don't think he would have come this morning, do you?" Andy was surprised at Jason's suggestion.

"No. I mean, I don't know, maybe he could have come this morning. Or maybe we just missed a clue," Jason offered. "I know we looked closely before. But it is possible that we missed something. What do you say?"

"Sure, that would be fine with me," Andy assented. So down the path the boys walked. They talked about how much fun it was to learn things from books.

"We need to remember to look up things in books when we have a mystery," Jason said. "Why, we may be able to solve mysteries even faster now that we know how to do book research."

Finally, they reached Dad's sign at the end of their property. Still, they hadn't found any new clues. They stood there for a minute, soaking up the sunshine and watching a few silly squirrels chase each other round and round a pine tree. "That looks like so much fun!" Andy said. "They never seem to get tired of chasing each other."

Jason agreed. "They sure don't seem to be worried about anything, either. I would think they should be gathering nuts for the cold days. Instead, they are just having fun!"

"I wonder if there are many nuts left around here anyway?" Andy asked. He kicked some leaves away and began to look on the path for fallen acorns from the nearby oak tree. "Sure, there's plenty left. Hey squirrels! You better come over here and grab some nuts to hide." The squirrels stopped to listen to Andy make this statement, chattered at him, then resumed their chasing fun. Both boys laughed.

"I guess they aren't as worried about the winter as you are, Andy. Maybe we should help them out some." Jason dropped down and began to gather some nuts into a pile. "Hey squirrels! We're doing your work for you. Don't you think you should come help?" This time the squirrels didn't even stop their play to listen.

It was so peaceful and warm in the woods that the boys didn't want to leave. Andy started gathering nuts for the squirrels, too. He added his to Jason's pile, and before long the pile was noticeably large.

While moving some leaves off the path, right near the Nelson property line, Andy noticed an old piece of string. Just as most boys would, Andy picked it up. That is, he started picking it up. As he stood up and tugged at the end of the string, he noticed that it was quite long. He continued to tug and could see movement under the leaves on the path. The more he tugged, the easier it was to see the length of the string. Finally he started reeling in the string. It had some resistance, like something was attached to its end or it was stuck under a rock. He jerked a little and the string loosened up from whatever had been holding it back. He continued to reel it in and estimated that he

The Mysterious Message

had already recovered about eight feet of string. Andy noticed something moving under the leaves ahead, as he reeled. *It must be the end of the string*, he thought to himself. *But why is it causing the leaves to lift off the ground?* Then he had another thought. *Maybe there is something attached to the end of this string.* He reeled faster and soon saw that indeed something was attached to the string's end. Andy looked over at Jason who was still gathering nuts and talking to the squirrels.

The end of the string was tied to an envelope. It was an ordinary envelope like many Andy had seen at his house. It had a little window in the front so that one could see the letter's address from the outside. Dad got a lot of them when companies sent him bills.

Andy was excited. He picked up the envelope and read through the little window these words: Wow! I'm surprised you found this one. Congratulations!!

"Jason, I've found it!" Andy called.

Jason ran over to his brother and looked at the envelope. "Have you opened it yet?"

"No, I just picked it up," Andy explained, opening the envelope and pulling a sheet of folded paper out. He read its contents out loud:

"Who are you? What are you up to?" I believe it was Andy who asked me those questions last night. That was you, wasn't it Andy? Those are good questions. Very soon you will learn the answers to them. Can hardly wait? Neither can I! Do you have any ideas? Probably not. Do you like chicken? I do. Wouldn't that be a treat? What's your favorite bird? Mine is the

Cactus Wren. Okay, I've said too much. See you Sat.
geb

"This is just so weird," exclaimed Jason. "Let's go back to our office and try to make some sense out of all of these clues."

"I'm with you," Andy agreed.

With that, the boys walked back to their house. Mom pulled in the driveway just about that time and the boys readily helped her unload the groceries and other things from the car.

After carrying two loads into the house, Jason suddenly exclaimed, "We've solved the Case of the Missing Bees! I forgot to tell you."

Cathy laughed at Jason's enthusiasm. "Well, tell us all about it. How did you solve it, guys?"

Jason and Andy filled Mom, Cathy, and Ben in on their book discoveries of the morning. Andy couldn't resist also telling some neat things he had seen and learned about the clipper ship *Flying Cloud*. As they related about the slips of paper, Cathy smiled and said, "So you found my notes."

"It was you!" Andy exclaimed. "If you knew the solution to the case, why did you ever 'hire' us to solve it?" Andy was confused.

"But I didn't know the solution," Cathy confessed. "I'm afraid I didn't even think of looking in our books for an answer until Dad mentioned something about it at supper last night. Then after you two went to bed, I looked up everything I could on skunks. I didn't know the solution until last night after you were in bed. I was going to tell you at breakfast, but decided to give you the morning to see if you could solve it on your own. Then, before I left to go to the store with Mom, I put those little slips of paper in the books."

"What if we hadn't solved it?" Jason wondered. "Would you have told us?"

"But you did!" Cathy exclaimed. "If you hadn't solved it this morning, I was going to help you discover it this afternoon. We do need to get the bee hives higher off the ground before tonight."

"So, Cathy solved her own mystery," Ben laughed. "That's funny."

"Actually the boys **also** solved my mystery, without help from me or anyone else," Cathy corrected Ben gently.

"I guess you're right," Ben agreed. Then he began to jump around the room, with his hands over his head, chanting, "The mystery is solved! The mystery is solved!"

"You certainly made Ben happy," Mom laughed. "I'm going to put away these groceries, then I'll begin putting lunch together. Why don't you go outside and enjoy the day? I'll call you when it's time to get washed up for lunch. It is a beautiful morning!"

"Yes ma'am," her children answered.

"I guess we can discuss the Case of the Mysterious Message outside just as easily as we can inside," Andy commented. He, Jason, and Ben walked to where Dad was splitting wood.

Seeing Ben, Dad said, "I guess Mom is home. I'm going in for a glass of water."

"We'll start stacking the split wood, Dad," Jason volunteered. "We can work while we talk."

As Dad walked into the house, the boys started

talking about the Case of the Mysterious Message. "Well, I'm convinced that he always comes at night," Andy began. "And isn't that a little scary how he heard me ask those questions last night? He must have been just inside the woods while I asked them. I wonder why we didn't see him when we were taking our walk down the path?"

"Maybe because it was too dark," Jason suggested, "and we didn't see where he was standing or sitting. Or maybe he was following along behind us and we just never heard him."

"Anyway, he did hear me ask those questions. It just looks like he might be spying on us or something," Andy said.

"But everything else we've seen seems to suggest that he is just trying to give us clues to make us wonder who he is," Jason disagreed. "I think if he were spying on us, he wouldn't leave us any clues at all. He would just spy and then quietly slip away, hopefully undetected."

Andy thought about that. "That does make sense," he said. "What was that about chicken?"

Jason took the sheet out of his pocket and read it again. "He asks if we like chicken and then tells us that he does. Then he says something about chicken being a treat."

"I think chicken is a treat!" noted Ben, who was helping stack the smaller pieces of wood. Andy and Jason often had to re-stack pieces of wood that Ben put on the woodpile, because they would be sticking out of the end of the stack too far or would be facing the wrong direction. Still, it was nice that Ben wanted to work and do his share.

The Mysterious Message

"All of this information about food is confusing to me. Why does he keep talking about food?" Andy asked. "The mysterious messenger said we might be eating peas. But Mom said they're not on our menu."

"Well, if Mom isn't planning on serving peas, I don't know how we are going to be able to eat them soon," Jason noted. "That is, unless we ask Mom to have them, or go get some out of the cupboard and just eat them as a snack."

The boys had almost finished stacking the wood that Dad had split. "Andy, you know we do have his initials now. He has signed the last two clues with 'geb.' At least I assume they're his initials. Do we know anyone with those initials? I've been trying to think of who it could be and keep drawing a blank."

"I've been trying to think about that myself. Of course, I am sure it must be his initials. It is at the end of each message. And it's three letters, which is what initials always have. But I was wondering if it could stand for something else. Like maybe a secret clue. It's similar to his always using the abbreviation 'Sat.' Is he doing that on purpose to give us some clue? We know it probably means Saturday. Then why doesn't he just spell out 'Saturday?' Why does he always use the abbreviated 'Sat'?"

"If it's not his initials, do you know what it could represent?" Jason asked.

Andy shook his head. "I don't have a clue, Jason. I have turned over lots of phrases in my mind but nothing seems to make sense. I mean, I thought of things like 'get every bee'." He wiped some dirt off his jeans and stretched his back. Working with wood can be tough on a back, even a young one. "I guess if we can't figure out any phrase that makes sense, we should assume that it stands for his initials." Then, feeling that he might have stumbled onto a good idea, he added, "Why don't we look in the phone book and see if that helps us any?"

Jason was not enthusiastic. "How many people have last names that begin with the letter 'b'? There must be hundreds just in our small town. Then we would have to see which of those people have first names that start with a 'g.' Even so, that might not help us much. If this is a boy, perhaps older than us but a boy just the same, his name wouldn't be listed in the phone book. Just his parents' names."

"You're right," Andy reluctantly agreed. His hopes for solving the mystery quickly were dashed.

"We could look in our family's little address book and see which family names start with a 'b'," offered Jason. "That shouldn't take too much time. Then we would know if they have a boy with a first name that starts with 'g.'"

Andy was suddenly feeling better about his earlier suggestion. "I'll look that up when I get inside. It must be about time to eat. Let's head in now." However, the boys continued to stand by the wood-pile, enjoying the warm morning.

"Yes," Ben chimed in. "I'm hungry. You guys should have come to the hardware store today. They had a man there showing people how to use some glues. He glued some plastic to a string, and then had some men hold the string while he tried to break it loose. It was neat!"

"That does sound like fun to watch," Andy said wistfully. "I hope he's still doing that when we go to

The Mysterious Message

the hardware store the next time."

"Nope," Ben corrected. "Mom said he was just there today. He is trying to get people to buy his glue."

"Too bad," Jason said. "Still, we had a pretty good time here at home this morning, didn't we partner?"

Andy nodded. Mom called from the doorway, "Wash up for lunch, guys. The pizza is ready!"

Chapter Eighteen

The boys walked into the house and began to wash their hands. While he was waiting his turn, Andy found the family's address book and looked under the letter 'B.' Reading down the list he saw many names that were quite familiar to him. Of course, some names he wasn't as familiar with; these were probably some of Mom's or Dad's old friends, business people, and people who had bought horses from the Nelsons. Dad raised Morgan horses and had been pretty successful in selling the horses he had personally trained.

The address book included the following last names starting with 'B': Basham, Becker, Bell, Berkshire, Bettner, Biel, Bogle, Bohannon, Blakely, Broome, two Browns, Burke, Burns, and Bush. Andy studied the names carefully. He thought of the children in the families whose names he recognized, yet none would have the initials 'geb.'

"Andy, please wash your hands quickly. It's time to eat," Mom said somewhat sternly. "We've been waiting on you."

"I'm sorry," Andy apologized as he rushed to the bathroom to wash his hands. Soon he was sitting down, ready for the blessing.

After the blessing, food was passed. Ben told the family all the details of the man at the hardware store who gave the demonstration. That man had obviously made quite an impression on Ben.

The Mysterious Message

"Did you buy some of his glue?" Dad asked Ben.

Ben looked perplexed. "No sir. I just watched the man play with his own glue."

During a break in the conversation, Andy turned to Jason. "I looked up the names in our phone directory. It didn't do any good. I didn't see any families I knew who would have children with those initials."

Jason nodded. "It was worth a try, Andy. We'll just have to keep thinking."

"So, has The Great Detective Agency begun to formulate its questions for me?" Dad smiled, looking around the table.

"We haven't had time yet," Jason responded. "We're hoping to work with Cathy this afternoon. Maybe right after lunch. What do you say, Cathy?"

"I can meet with you about an hour after lunch," Cathy said. "I just have to get this blouse finished first."

"Dad, will you need our help this afternoon?" Jason asked.

"No, I'm going to chop some more wood," Dad replied.

"Whenever you are ready for us to stack, just let us know," Jason said. "We'll be in our office trying to solve the Case of the Mysterious Message."

When the boys arrived in their office, they had to take a few minutes to remove cobwebs and dust from the makeshift desk made from an old box. "Having an office under the stairs is hard on our furniture," Andy noted. "The dirt that gets swept into our office makes for a continuous mess." He had, at times, dreamed of having a nice, clean office with filing cabinets and real desks. Now, he looked around lovingly at all the little touches the boys had added to their office. He glanced at the calendar which had a different picture of a seeing eye dog each month. He then looked at the magnifying glass hanging on its nail, the sheet of construction paper outlining The Great Detective Agency's policies and procedures, the 3 x 5 card listing all of the cases they had successfully solved (sometimes with help), and the steel box which held their most important clues for safe keeping. The box had been given to them by their Uncle Bruce, who was a sergeant in the Marines. It was an old ammunition container. *No*, Andy thought to himself, *I wouldn't trade this place for any other.*

"Why don't we take a few minutes and just list all the clues we have for the Case of the Mysterious Message?" Jason suggested. "I have to admit that we've been so busy, I can't remember everything."

"That sounds like a good idea," Andy agreed, taking out his spiral notebook. "Do you want to make the list or should I?"

Jason leaned back in his chair. "Why don't you write down the list?" This was acceptable to Andy. Here is their list:

Wednesday

1. Found message in snow. Written with a glove or finger right in the snow. Said "I will see you Sat".
2. Found pile of rocks a few feet away from the message (the message written in the snow). Must have been made by same person who left the message.
3. Tracked footprints. Boots are larger than ours

The Mysterious Message

(probably an older boy or a man). Prints led all over the place, off the path, up a tree, and everywhere. Followed them to edge of property. They kept going past Dad's sign, but we couldn't (family rule).

4. Found more writing in snow. Said "Good job".

Thursday

1. Looked under pile of rocks. Didn't find anything there.
2. Walked down path and found a sapling cut across the path. With a saw! Looked up in tree and saw a piece of cardboard hanging up there.
3. Message on cardboard said that he knows about us and that we had better start learning about him. Told us that "Sat is coming soon." Used red marker to write these words. Pretty messy handwriting. Back side of cardboard had the letters "Del" on it, along with a little blue and red ink. Couldn't make out next letter for sure, but it looked like it had a straight up-and-down line as part of it.

Friday

1. Found small tin can near base of tree. Label had been torn off. Smelled like peas used to be in the can.
2. Found plastic bag underneath leaves under can. Note inside.
3. Note was in cursive writing. Letter praised us for finding it. Called us Nelson Detective Agency.

The Farm Mystery Series

Said we will see contents of can again, maybe even eat it. Said it was dark when he left the clue and that we will know him soon. Used initials of 'geb'.

Saturday

1. Found string on the ground in path near our property line. Pulled on string and found envelope at end of string.
2. Envelope was like the kind Dad gets with bills, with little cellophane window in it. Could read through the little window these words "Wow, I'm surprised you found this one. Congratulations!"
3. Note inside envelope said he knew what Andy said on Friday night. Knows Andy's name. Asked if we liked chicken. Said he does and thinks it's some kind of a treat. Cactus Wren is his favorite bird. Said he will see us on Sat. Signed initials with "geb" again.

"Boy, that's a lot of clues, for us not to have any better idea of who he is or what he's up to," Jason said.

Andy had a thought. "This is Saturday. Do you think something is going to happen today?"

Jason had already thought of that. "It's possible. Of course, the clues don't say on what Saturday we might meet him. It could be this weekend or next weekend or any Saturday in the future. For some reason, I just don't think it's going to be today."

"Maybe you're right," Andy agreed. "Still, we ought to keep our eyes open pretty well today just in

The Mysterious Message

case. It may be that we will see him, but not realize it's him because we're not really looking for him, if you know what I mean."

"I wish I knew what that 'Del' stands for. The way this guy is always trying to leave us clues makes me think that it wasn't just coincidence that he let that be on the back of his note," Jason said. "But maybe I'm trying to find a clue where there really isn't one. This one just has me stumped!"

"I wonder if maybe he left several of those clues at the same time," Andy thought out loud. "Just because we found them on different days doesn't mean he left them on different days. That tin can and the note underneath it could have been there on Wednesday morning for all we know. We might have just over-looked it."

Jason hadn't thought of that. "Yeah," he said with enthusiasm. "Sure, that's possible. Of course that last clue tied to the string had to be fresh today because it referred to what you said last night."

"I hadn't thought of that," Andy admitted. "And I wonder why he is telling us about little things. You know, like his favorite bird and what he likes to eat. How is that going to help us learn who he is? Should we start knocking on doors in the neighborhood asking people if they like to eat chicken and get suspicious if they do?"

Jason laughed at that. "Yes. Or we could see who has a picture of a Cactus Wren on his wall as we talk to people in their doorways. What is a Cactus Wren anyway?"

"I don't know," Andy said. "I know what a wren is. There are many different kinds of wrens. But I'm not sure what a Cactus one would be."

"Maybe it's one that doesn't have to take a drink very often," laughed Jason.

Andy laughed too. "Or maybe it's one that has prickly feathers sticking out of it!"

Both boys laughed for a few minutes, thinking of birds with crazy features that could somehow be called Cactus. Jason laughed so hard that he fell off his chair and sent the small table (which was actually a cardboard box) sailing into the side wall. That made Andy laugh and drop his pencil. The pencil just happened to land in the empty pea can. Naturally, that got the boys even more tickled.

"Well, I suppose we should go up and see if Cathy has finished with her blouse," Andy said after a few minutes. The boys straightened up their office, closed their notebooks, and turned off the flashlight that was dangling from a string above the 'desk'. Andy looked back with admiration at the tiny office. It sure was a neat place.

Chapter Nineteen

Cathy was in the living room, sewing the last buttons onto her new blue striped blouse. "I was just thinking that you guys should be coming up soon," she commented. "I'm ready to meet with you. It will be easy for me to sew on these last few buttons while we discuss what we know and what our next step should be."

"I think the answer to the Case of the Missing Gas lies in the idea that somehow the gas has reappeared," Jason offered. "Although Dad said that it was possible that someone was stealing the gas during the day, his answers last night didn't make me think that was the solution."

"Why?" asked Andy. "I thought that was still a possibility. There is a pump on the tank, and it pumps really fast. I don't think it would take long for someone to drive in, fill up an empty tank in the back of a pickup, and then drive away."

"While all of that is true, I tend to agree with Jason," Cathy replied. "Dad said that there are a number of men whose job at the mill keeps them moving around sort of randomly all day. Whoever was going to steal the gas would certainly have to be concerned about that. It would take someone pretty bold to drive up and steal some gas, knowing that Dad or someone else might come around the corner at any minute. They would be caught red-handed."

The Farm Mystery Series

Andy listened to Cathy's reasoning, but was still not convinced. "Dad didn't say we were on the wrong track. I think we should still consider it as a possibility." Then, realizing that his views were not in the majority, he added, "But I guess we should look at the other possibility a little more closely first."

"Good," Jason approved, smiling at his partner. "Now, in what different ways could the gas have 'reappeared?' And when I say that, we all know that I mean that it either reappeared or never was missing in the first place."

Cathy tied a knot in her thread, then answered, "One possibility is that Mr. Popper read the measurement wrong; either the first time he read the meter, or later, when he read the meter and thought that someone was stealing his gas. I suppose that is possible. Especially since Dad told us Mr. Popper read the meter right before he left for the night. Maybe he was tired. Then, when he read it the next time, Dad said it was early in the morning. Maybe it wasn't fully light. In both cases, it would be easy to make a mistake."

Jason thought about that. "That's true," he admitted. "I guess we've all done something like that sometime during our life. But if he did read it wrong, I would think he only misread it when he took the first reading. When he took his last reading and realized that so much gas was missing, I would expect he would immediately look at the gauge again just to check himself. You know, like 'Wow, is that really what the meter reads?' (he would say, turning around to take a second look to verify what he just found out). See what I mean?"

"I do," Andy offered. "I agree that his last reading

The Mysterious Message

couldn't be the one that he misread."

"True enough," Cathy said, "but only if he instantly realized that his last reading was actually so far out of bounds. What if he just wrote it down, though, and later realized that it was way off?"

"I would think he would march right out and check the meter again," Jason suggested.

Cathy agreed. "Okay, reading the meter wrongly at first may be one solution. What's another one?"

The three sat in silence trying to think of other solutions. Finally, Andy spoke up. "Maybe someone **was** stealing the gas. After Mr. Popper made a big deal about the gas being gone, the person who stole it found out, got afraid he might get caught, and just pumped it back into the tank. That would explain why Dad let us think that both solutions were possible."

Jason and Cathy thought about that possibility. "That is possible, Andy," Cathy said. "Of course, we have the same problem that we had with someone stealing the gas during the day. It would be just as risky to try and pump the gas back into the tank during the day as it was to pump it out in the first place. Also, the person would have to have some kind of pump to pump the gas back into the mill's tank. I don't know how easy that would be."

Jason tried to think of some new angle. "Well, let's say that Mr. Popper didn't make any mistake in reading the gauge and that no one stole the gas. How else could it have reappeared?"

Everyone thought about Jason's question. The room was silent for quite a while.

"The gas level could be returned to where it should be because the gas company delivered more gas to the mill," Jason finally offered.

"But wouldn't Mr. Popper know that? Why would the gas company try to hide that fact?" Cathy questioned.

"I didn't mean that they would hide it," Jason explained. "What if there was some kind of a leak in the tank that was the fault of the gas company? Then the gas company would be responsible for not only repairing the leak, but also for replacing the lost gas. That would explain how the gas reappeared, yet wasn't stolen." Jason felt pretty good about his suggestion.

"What was Dad's answer when we asked him if Mr. Popper somehow made a mistake when measuring the gas?" Cathy asked. "He said 'yes and no.' If what you are suggesting is the solution to the case, Jason, then how could Mr. Popper have made some mistake reading the gauge?"

Jason didn't know the answer to Cathy's question. In fact, he was getting a little confused.

"What **did** Dad mean when he told us 'yes and no'?" Andy asked. "That didn't make sense to me last night."

Cathy placed the finished blouse beside her on the couch. "I'm not exactly sure what he meant by that." She hesitated. "It usually means that there is some truth to what was said, but that what was said is not the whole story. Let me give you an example. Suppose a blind man, using a cane, accidently knocks over an expensive vase that is placed on a low shelf in a department store. When the storekeeper takes the blind man to court, the judge asks the blind man, 'Are you responsible for breaking the vase?' The blind man would probably say, 'Yes, and no. I did knock it over, but I'm not responsible for it since I am blind and couldn't see it."

Cathy looked at the boys to see if they were understanding what she was explaining. They seemed to, so she continued. "So in this case, it could mean that Mr. Popper did, to some extent, make a mistake in how he read the meter, but that maybe the mistake was outside of his control."

"I understand!" Andy nodded. "Boy, you're good at explaining things, Cathy!" After a moment, he added, "But what things could have been outside of his control? Mr. Popper isn't blind."

"That has been puzzling me since last night," admitted Cathy.

After much discussion they agreed on the following questions: "Did Mr. Popper read the meter wrong the first time he read it?" "Was the tank leaking, and since the gas company was responsible for the leak, the gas company fixed the leak and delivered more fuel for free?" "Was someone stealing the gas, got afraid, and then replaced it in the tank while no one was looking?"

"What else should we ask?" Andy questioned.

"I just don't know," Jason replied. "Any ideas, Cathy?"

"No, I really don't have any," Cathy admitted.

Just then Dad walked into the living room. "So, here's the crew! Have you any questions for your old dad?"

"Yes sir," grinned Jason. Looking at Andy, he added, "Let's take turns asking the questions. First, is it possible that Mr. Popper just read the meter wrong? I mean, when he read the meter the first time, could he maybe have read it wrong and thought he had more gas than he actually did have?"

Dad smiled. "That's a good guess. But, no. Mr. Popper wrote down the reading and that is exactly what it was."

Andy jumped in. "Our next question is this: Could it be possible that someone was stealing gas? Then maybe they found out that Mr. Popper knew, and got afraid. So, they drove back and replaced the gas in your tank to keep from getting into trouble?"

"Lots of good ideas. Again, I suppose that is possible. It has certainly happened before. I've read of bank robbers who started feeling guilty or started thinking about spending the rest of their lives in jail who returned the money. One robber even sent it back through the mail," Dad grinned, "and included his return address. But that's not what happened in this case. How about another question?"

"It's my turn again," Jason said. "This may be hard to follow so I'll try to go slowly. What if your tank really did have a leak in it? That would explain why the reading was so low. Then, when Mr. Popper called the gas company, they came out, fixed the leak in the tank, and then replaced the gas that had leaked. So, you could say that the gas sort of did reappear and yet didn't exactly reappear, if you know what I mean. The free gas from the gas company would obviously be new to your mill, not the gas that escaped into the air."

"I see what you're saying," Dad replied. "Sorry to disappoint you, though. There really is no leak in the tank. What's your last question?"

The Mysterious Message

"We really don't have another one, Dad," Andy said. "I think we've just about exhausted our ideas."

Dad got a gleam in his eyes and said, "Follow me, crew! It's time for a home schooling lesson." He then marched into the kitchen and opened the bottom drawer of Mom's old-fashioned kitchen cupboard. He pulled out a bag of balloons and carefully selected three pink ones.

"Hey, what are you going to do with those balloons, Dad?" Ben asked excitedly. "It's not someone's birthday, is it?"

"You'll see," was all Dad would say. After stretching a balloon, he blew it up, then picked up another one. It appeared he was taking great pains to make sure each was the same size.

By this time, Mom had joined the group watching Dad. "What is he doing?" she asked Cathy.

"I don't know," Cathy giggled. "Maybe he's going to teach us how to play with balloons."

That caused Dad to laugh and lose most of the air out of the third balloon. However, he blew it back up to the same size as the other two. Then he placed them on the kitchen table. "Cathy, please turn the oven on, to say, 250°. Jason, you can carefully get Mom's glass casserole baking dish. And Ben, please find me a wooden clothes pin." Everyone started moving and smiling with happiness. It was so much fun when Dad taught them things. "Andy, could you clear off one shelf in the freezer? Just move things around to the other shelves." Dad stood watching his family carry out his wishes.

When they had completed their tasks, the children lined up and stood at attention. Dad laughed again.

"Well, I can see I have your undivided attention. Look at the table. What do you see?" he asked.

"Three balloons!" Ben answered quickly.

"Nothing made for supper yet," Mom interjected, laughing.

"Focus on the balloons for now," Dad instructed her, laughing with Mom. "Notice that they are all the same size. You children pick them up and feel them. See if they all seem to be filled up about the same amount."

The children obeyed. "They seem to be the same," Jason said. "But I don't understand . . ."

Before he could finish, Dad said, "You will soon." Then addressing Cathy, he asked, "Is the oven pre-heated yet?"

Cathy looked at the thermostat. "Yes sir, it's ready."

Dad picked up a balloon and walked in the direction of the stove. He passed it however, opened the freezer door, and placed one balloon on the empty shelf.

Words can't describe how curious this made the children. Dad saw their expressions and couldn't resist laughing again. Then he grabbed another balloon and opened the oven door. "Cathy, please hand me the casserole dish now and the clothes pin." Dad clipped the clothes pin onto the end of the balloon, placed the balloon inside the casserole dish, and slid the dish into the oven, closing the door. Then he turned on the oven light and said, "Gather round and tell me what happens.

Everyone looked through the smoked glass into the oven. The balloon was just sitting in there, apparently baking.

"Is this what you've been wanting for supper?" Mom asked Dad.

Before he could answer, a pop was heard, and Andy exclaimed, "Hey Dad, you better come here. Your balloon just blew up!"

Dad raced to the stove and pulled out the fragments of the balloon. One had dropped onto the heating element and was already smoking. Dad looked at Mom, a little embarrassed. "Sorry, I'll clean that up later."

Then, with the smell of burning rubber starting to fill the air, he addressed his children. "Why did the balloon explode?"

"Because it is hot in the oven," Jason offered.

"Yes, but why did that explode it?" Dad probed.

Cathy had been thinking. "I know," she said. "It's because the air inside the balloon expanded. The balloon got bigger and bigger, and then when it couldn't get any bigger, it just exploded."

Ben was excited. "Can we blow up another balloon, Dad?"

Dad looked at Mom, who had opened a window to let the burning rubber smell escape. "I guess not," Dad said. "Let's learn from this little experiment. When air is heated up it expands, which just means it gets bigger. Okay?"

"Sure," Andy said.

"Now, what do you think would happen to air when it got cold?"

"It would contract, or get smaller," Cathy answered. "Which means our balloon in the freezer should be smaller than it was."

Jason ran to the freezer and picked up the balloon. He then took it to the table and compared it to the third balloon that was still sitting there. "It doesn't look a lot different," he said, "although it does seem to be a little looser."

"Well, to have an equally quick reaction to the one in the oven, we would have to have a much colder freezer," Dad suggested. "We would need to lower the temperature instantly by about 180 degrees, which isn't possible. But can you see that heat and cold does have an effect on air?"

"Yes sir," all agreed, even Ben.

"Well, air, which is just a gas, acts like all other gases. When any gas is heated, it expands. When a gas is cooled, it contracts, which means it gets smaller. That is what happened at the mill!"

Jason and Andy were still puzzled.

"I'll try to explain," Dad began. "What happened at the mill is this. John took a reading on the tank when it was rather warm outside, in mid-October. You know how it was unseasonably hot that week. That's when you guys helped me wash and wax my truck.

"Well, when he took his next reading, the temperature had fallen about sixty degrees. The gas inside the tank got cold. When it got cold, it contracted. As a result, the gas meter said that John had lost about 10 percent of his gas."

"Where did the gas go?" asked Jason.

"It didn't go anywhere," Dad said. "It just contracted. John didn't know this was even a possibility until he called the gas company. They assured him it was nothing at all to worry about. In fact, they have charts showing how much the gas shrinks, depending

The Mysterious Message

on the temperature. At 60°F there is no shrinkage. If the temperature drops from 60° to 0°F, the gas shrinks by about 9%. It works the other way also. If the temperature rises from 60° to 100°F, the gas expands by 7%!"

"That doesn't seem fair," Ben said. "The gas company is cheating you when it gets cold outside."

"You might think so." Dad smiled at Ben. "Actually, though it may be hard to understand, that's not the case. Even though the gas shrinks, you still have the same volume of gas. So it will still run the same number of tow trucks, for example."

Dad popped the last two balloons and Ben squealed with delight.

"You boys certainly did a great job thinking of questions," Dad commented. "You too, Cathy. It's fun when we all work together and use the brains that God blessed us with. Godly wisdom is much more important than mere knowledge, however." Then picking up a Bible that was lying on the table, he turned to the book of Proverbs, Chapter three. "Let's remember what God has to say about wisdom." After reading the passage, Dad explained what it meant. The Nelson children were always ready to listen when Dad explained what the Bible had to say.

Chapter Twenty

The rest of the afternoon the boys played together. They also helped Dad do odd jobs around the farm. Late in the afternoon Dad brought some concrete blocks and placed the bee hives on top of several layers of block. "That should frustrate our skunk friends," Dad said. "Maybe our bee losses will end."

"Boys, you need to go ahead and do chores," Mom called out to the boys. "We are going to do something special tonight."

The boys walked to the barn, all excited by this news. "Did you know we were going to do anything neat tonight?" Jason asked Andy.

"No, not until Mom just now said it," Andy replied. "I wonder what's going on?"

Ben spoke up. "I think I know." Since little brothers sometimes know these kinds of things, for a variety of reasons, both older boys stopped walking.

"What are we going to do, Ben?" Jason asked. "Do you really know?"

"I think we're going to go and buy a new horse!" Ben whispered, looking back toward the house as he said it.

"Neat!" Andy exclaimed.

The boys did their chores quickly. It's amazing how fast boys can work if something fun is coming up. As they were walking back to the house, Andy said,

The Mysterious Message

"Say, maybe we should look for any more clues to the Case of the Mysterious Message. What do you think?"

"I'll ask Mom if we have time," Jason said. In a minute he was back out of the house. "She said we didn't have time. And that we need to come right in and get changed. We're going somewhere but she didn't say where!"

The boys got washed up and changed into the clothes that Mom suggested. Soon everyone was in the car, heading down the highway.

"When will you tell us where we're going?" asked Jason.

"Yes," pleaded Andy. Ben just sat there with a satisfied look on his face.

Dad looked at Mom and smiled. "Oh, I guess you guys will find out in about two minutes," Dad said.

Andy held up two fingers to Jason with a questioning look on his face. Jason just shrugged his shoulders as if to say, "I don't know how it can only take two minutes."

Sure enough, in just a few minutes, Dad turned off the highway into a driveway. The older boys craned their necks, trying to figure out what was going on. Ben continued to sit still, looking straight ahead, quite confident that he knew what was going on. It was Cathy who spoke first. "This is the Browns' house, isn't it Dad?"

"Yes it is," Dad replied. It was getting dark outside and Dad turned his lights on as he continued down the long, winding driveway through heavy woods. Finally, he pulled the car to a stop and turned off the lights. "Okay," he said, opening his door, "let's go have some supper."

As they were getting out of the car, a porch light turned on and the side door opened. Out walked Mr. and Mrs. Brown. "Welcome, Timothy, Connie, Cathy, . . . boys," Mr. Brown smiled, walking toward the car.

As greetings were exchanged, Ben seemed a little hesitant. "You remember Mr. Brown, don't you, Ben?" Dad said, holding Ben's hand.

"No sir," Ben said a little shyly.

"Now, you should remember me," boomed Mr. Brown. "Especially after I gave you a ride on my tractor just last year, when I helped your dad put up his hay."

That seemed to thaw out Ben quite a bit. He let go of Dad's hand and said, "Are you selling a horse?"

Mr. Brown looked confused. "Should I?" he asked, grinning.

Ben didn't answer because Mrs. Brown was telling everyone to come in.

As they finished taking off their jackets, a boy appeared in the doorway. "There you are," said Mrs. Brown. "I've been wondering where you've been."

"I was in the basement," the boy answered. "I'm sorry, Aunt Sadie."

"I would like to introduce my nephew, Gideon Brown," Mr. Brown said. "He is visiting with us for most of the month of December. He's from Phoenix, Arizona."

"It's nice to meet you," Dad returned politely. "Let me introduce my family." Dad then introduced the members of his family, and included the children's ages. "How old are you, Gideon?"

The Mysterious Message

"I'm sixteen," he said. "But I'll be seventeen in January."

"Sorry we're running a little late, Sadie," Mom said. "I hope we haven't messed up your meal in some way."

"Now don't you worry about a thing," Mrs. Brown said. "The chicken just came out of the oven a few minutes ago. I think we are all set and ready for you to find your seats."

Soon everyone was seated. After Mr. Brown led in prayer, the food was passed around the table. Andy sat up straight as he eyed the delicious dishes before him. Fried chicken with potato salad was one of his favorites. And he was just sure that he smelled a pumpkin pie back in the kitchen somewhere. This was a treat. He looked over at Jason, who winked at him.

"So, is this your first trip to Tennessee, Gideon?" Dad asked.

"Yes sir," Gideon replied. "It's really nice here. That snow the other day was pretty fun. I don't get much chance to be out in snow."

"What kinds of things are you going to do while you're here?" Mom asked.

"Uncle Ralph and Aunt Sadie are going to take me up to the Smoky Mountains. I look forward to that. Also, we're going to visit some of my relatives in Chattanooga."

"That sounds like fun," Dad said. "You better listen to the weather forecast, Ralph, before heading up to Gatlinburg. When it snows up there it can be pretty treacherous, you know. I was up there once when they got no more than four inches. But I guess it took me three hours just to get down from the mountains. The roads were so bad that the traffic was crawling!"

"I'll keep that in mind, Timothy," Mr. Brown responded. "I've never been to the Smokies in the winter time. Probably wouldn't hurt to throw a few coats in the car, either!"

Gideon was seated next to Andy. Looking at Andy's plate, he smiled and asked, "Can I pass you some peas?"

"Not right now, thanks," Andy said.

"How about you, Jason? Would you like some peas?" Gideon asked.

"Sure, I'll take some." Jason paused as he placed the peas on his plate. It seemed odd to have peas so soon again. Hadn't they had them at home just recently?

After this exchange, Gideon addressed Andy again. "How did you like the snow we got on Wednesday? Did you do anything fun?"

There was something odd about the way that Gideon asked that question. But try as he might, Andy couldn't figure out what it was.

"It was fun just to be in it," Andy answered honestly. "We don't get snow here as often as we would like, so we enjoy it as much as we can."

"I'm sure you do," Gideon said. Then turning to Cathy, he asked, "Where do you go to school?"

"We home school," Cathy said.

"Oh, I've heard of that," Gideon said. "That sounds like fun. I go to a private school back in Phoenix. It's one of the top schools in the state as far as academics go."

The Mysterious Message

"That's nice," Cathy said.

Dad began to talk to Mr. Brown about water pipes in the barn. The recent cold spell had caused trouble for many farmers in the area with frozen pipes. Mr. Brown had had his share of troubles during the cold spell.

"My biggest problem was in trying to get my tractor started," Mr. Brown stated. "It wouldn't start and I probably overcompensated by giving it too much gas. Must have gotten flooded. Once that happened there was no way to get the thing started. When I pulled the spark plugs, each cylinder was loaded with gas. What a mess!"

Dad laughed, as one who well knew these kinds of trials.

"That gas would not evaporate. So guess what I did?" Mr. Brown asked, directing his question at Jason.

"I don't know," Jason answered dutifully.

"I borrowed Sadie's hair dryer and blew hot air into each cylinder. Dried them up, too!" Mr. Brown led everyone at the table in a round of laughter. "I always knew there must be some good use I could put a hair dryer to," he added, rubbing his bald head for everyone's amusement. "Of course," he said seriously, "that wasn't a very wise thing to do. The hair dryer could have easily ignited the gas fumes! Don't you boys ever try anything like that."

After supper, the boys wandered into the living room with Gideon while the adults talked around the table. Cathy insisted on helping Mrs. Brown by starting on the supper dishes.

"What's it like to live in Phoenix?" asked Andy.

"I've always heard it's pretty hot in Arizona."

"We sure get our share of the heat!" Gideon replied. "In the summer, it can get up to 110° easily."

At the amazed looks of the boys, Gideon continued. "Of course, we make up for it with our mild winters. In Phoenix, where I live, it almost never freezes and we don't get snow."

"I guess you mostly get rain," Jason suggested.

"Actually, not much of that either," Gideon corrected. "I'd say we don't get eight inches of rain in a whole year. Mostly it's clear in Phoenix."

"Wow," remarked Andy. "That's sure a lot different from here."

"Did your daddy drive you here?" questioned Ben. "Arizona must be a long way away!"

"No, I flew on an airplane," Gideon said. "That was my first flight. Have you guys ever flown with Delta Airlines?" He didn't address anyone by name, yet seemed to be focusing on Andy.

Why's he looking at me? Andy thought to himself. *I haven't ever flown on an airplane!*

Jason answered for the trio. "We haven't flown in an airplane, but we would sure like to. Dad says that when you take off, the speed causes you to be pushed back in your seat. That would be neat!"

Ben loved this conversation and expressed his excitement accordingly. "Did you get on top of the clouds?" he asked.

"Yes, we flew high above the clouds. Part of the trip was at night, so I can only speculate on where we were then," Gideon answered. Changing the subject, he asked, "Wasn't that a good supper we had? Aunt Sadie's fried chicken and potato salad are hard to beat.

The Mysterious Message

And pumpkin pie is a real treat, too."

"It was great," all the boys agreed.

As the room got quiet, it suddenly seemed uncomfortable. It was as though no one knew what to say or do next. Gideon sat on the edge of the couch, tossing a ball of yarn back and forth between his hands, apparently in thought.

I wonder if he misses home, Andy thought. Then trying to cheer up Gideon, he asked, "Do you have much wildlife in Arizona? We have coyotes here."

Gideon thought for a minute. "Yes, we have lots of wildlife. A lot of reptiles. Boy, do we have the snakes!" After a minute, he continued, "But my favorites are the birds. We have this one bird that is called the 'Cactus Wren' and it is so . . ."

As Gideon was talking, Jason found it hard to concentrate on what the older boy was saying. His mind was fuzzy for some reason. He tried to back up, and remember what the conversation had just been. He remembered Andy mentioning coyotes and Gideon talking about snakes. Birds. Cactus Wren! That was what was bothering Jason. The clue in the woods had mentioned Cactus Wren also.

Jason looked at Andy. Andy had a strange look on his face. Not wanting to be impolite, since Gideon was still talking, Jason didn't speak. However, he gave a nonverbal message to Andy that said, "Keep your eyes and ears open, Andy! There's something going on here!"

When Gideon stopped talking, Jason asked, "Where do Cactus Wrens live?"

"I'm not exactly sure what their habitat is," Gideon answered. "But I know we have them in Arizona. In fact, they are our state bird."

Jason was thinking hard. What were the other clues in the Case of the Mysterious Message? Something about peas and chicken. And mention of Cactus Wrens.

Before Jason could speak, however, Andy asked a question. "This may sound like a silly question, Gideon, but what is your middle name?"

Gideon looked surprised. "My middle name? That is an odd question! Why do you want to know?" Gideon looked at Andy as though he had lost his mind. Andy was beginning to think that maybe he had. He was embarrassed for asking the question in such a direct way.

"Oh, I just wondered," Andy replied. "Of course, if you don't want to tell it, that's okay, too. Some people don't like their middle names."

Gideon laughed. Then looking from Andy to Jason, he answered. "I'm not embarrassed. My middle name is Edward. Gideon Edward Brown. I was named for my great-grandfather."

Andy's heart was pounding. He, like Jason, had been thinking of the Case of the Mysterious Message just as soon as Gideon had mentioned the Cactus Wren. All the clues seemed to point to Gideon as their mysterious messenger. Yet, even though Andy had asked about his middle name, Gideon wasn't admitting that it was him. *What should I do now?* thought Andy. Looking at Jason, he saw that Jason had the same idea.

Finally, Jason spoke up. "We have been having this mysterious . . . Well, what I mean is that someone has left us some messages . . ." Jason was having trouble bringing up the subject. Gideon looked at Jason, listening patiently, but giving no cues that suggested he knew anything about the Case of the Mysterious Message.

Andy finally finished for Jason. "We have been having a mysterious visitor to our property. He's been leaving us messages for the last four days. Do you know anything about it?"

Gideon looked at Andy, then at Jason, then back at Andy again. He started laughing. Jason and Andy didn't know how to interpret this outburst.

When he controlled himself again, Gideon said, "Yes, guys, I'm your mysterious messenger. My uncle told me how much you all liked mysteries. I love mysteries myself. I thought it would be fun to sort of give you a mystery to solve. I knew that we were going to be eating supper with your family tonight and so I gave you clues to think about. I hope I didn't scare you or anything."

Neither Jason nor Andy could reply for a minute. Then Jason looked up with a smile. "It's great! It all makes sense now. Don't you see, Andy? It almost had to be someone who lived close by, but we couldn't think of anybody who could be doing this. Of course, we didn't even know that Gideon was visiting here at the Browns' house."

"Sure, and we had peas and chicken for supper," Andy said. "But what did 'Del' stand for on the back of the cardboard?"

"Delta Airlines!" Gideon informed them. "It came off the garment box they gave me at the airport."

Both boys laughed. "Did you make the pile of rocks?" Jason asked.

"I am guilty!" Gideon laughed. "I hope it was okay. You really weren't scared or anything were you?" He was either genuinely concerned about the boys' welfare, or was afraid that he might get in trouble with his aunt and uncle for scaring their neighbors.

"No, we weren't too scared," Andy reassured him. "It was fun to try and figure it out." Then turning to Jason, he pulled his notebook out of his pocket. "The Case of the Mysterious Message is solved!"

Before long it was time for the Nelsons to leave. Thanking the Browns for the supper and the company, the boys said, "Good night." Then Jason warned, "And don't be surprised, Gideon, if some strange clues start coming your way in the next couple of weeks."

Gideon just laughed. "That would be fun!"

Chapter Twenty-one

When the family returned home, Mom made the inevitable statement, "It's late, boys. You need to get changed quickly so we can have our devotions. No fooling around, now. I want you all down here in five minutes." Then as the boys started disappearing up the steps she added, "And put your clothes away nicely."

"Yes ma'am," came three voices from upstairs.

When everyone was gathered in the living room, Dad picked up his Bible and read from John 16. "These verses warn us that persecution is something that may come our way, just because we're Christians," Dad explained. "Yet, praise God, He also gave us a Comforter. The Comforter is, of course, the Holy Spirit. As we pray, let's thank God for providing us with the true Comforter.

"There's something else we need to pray about," Dad continued. He looked at Mom and smiled. "Mom and I have been praying about something for quite a while now. We feel that the Lord is leading us to adopt several children into our family. We didn't want to tell you until we knew that God was really leading us in that direction."

Almost instantly he was surrounded with questions. "When will we adopt the children?" "Do we know them already?" "How many children will we adopt?" "How old are they?" "What does adopt

153

. mean?" " Will they sleep in our room?" Dad waved his hand for silence.

"Hold on, crew!" he said laughing. "You're asking a lot of questions, most of which we can't answer right now. But I know I can answer Ben's question. To adopt a child means that we will be able to give a home and family to a child who does not have one. They would become one of our children, just like you are. Does that make sense?"

"Sure," Ben said. "I'd have a new brother to play with!"

"Or sister," Dad added. "Or both. In fact, we have already learned of a little brother and sister who need to be adopted. They no longer have any parents alive and need a loving home."

"When can we get them?" Jason asked with excitement.

"Well, we will just have to wait and see if it is in the Lord's will," Dad said. "Actually, the possibility of adopting these two children is very exciting for us. They are living in a country where Christians are being persecuted right now. We would be able to raise them and tell them about Jesus. That is something that might not happen where they are now."

It took a few minutes for those words to sink in. Finally, Jason said, "Neat! We've been praying for God to show us how we could help people in persecuted countries. This could really be a way to help!"

The family had a time of prayer. As they rose, everyone was happy and excited. Mom looked at the clock and said, "Oh, Timothy! Do you see what time it is?"

"That's okay," Dad reassured her. "These kinds of

The Mysterious Message

days don't come along very often." After hugging everyone, Dad announced, "Time for bed, folks! Tomorrow is Sunday, and will be here very soon."

As Andy lay in bed, trying to settle down from the excitement of the evening, he thought about all that had happened in the last several days. He recounted the cases that The Great Detective Agency had worked on. The Case of the Missing Bees, the Case of the Missing Railroad, the Case of the Mysterious Message, and the Case of the Missing Gas. It had sure been busy. And fun. And now he might have a new brother and sister!

As he drifted off to sleep, a thought came to him: *I wonder if a new brother and sister would like mysteries?*

The End

Castleberry Farms Press

Our primary goal in publishing is to provide wholesome books in a manner that brings honor to our Lord. We believe in setting no evil thing before our eyes (Psalm 101:3) and although there are many outstanding books, we have had trouble finding enough good reading material for our children. Therefore, we feel the Lord has led us to start this family business.

We believe the following: The Bible is the infallible true Word of God. That God is the Creator and Controller of the universe. That Jesus Christ is the only begotten Son of God, born of the virgin Mary, lived a perfect life, was crucified, buried, rose again, sits at the right hand of God, and makes intercession for the saints. That Jesus Christ is the only Savior and way to the Father. That salvation is based on faith alone, but true faith will produce good works. That the Holy Spirit is given to believers as Guide and Comforter. That the Lord Jesus will return again. That man was created to glorify God and enjoy Him forever.

We began writing and publishing in mid-1996 and hope to add more books in the future if the Lord is willing. All books are written by Mr. and Mrs. Castleberry.

The Courtship Series

These books are written to encourage those who intend to follow a Biblically-based courtship that includes the active involvement of parents. The main characters are committed followers of Jesus Christ, and Christian family values are emphasized throughout. The reader will be encouraged to heed parental advice and to live in obedience to the Lord.

NEW! Jeff McLean: His Courtship

Follow the story of Jeff McLean as he seeks God's direction for his life. This book is the newest in our courtship series, and is written from a young man's perspective. A discussion of godly traits to seek in young men and women is included as part of the story. February 1998. Paperback. $7.50 (plus shipping and handling).

The Courtship of Sarah McLean

Sarah McLean is a nineteen year-old girl who longs to become a wife and mother. The book chronicles a period of two years, in which she has to learn to trust her parents and God fully in their decisions for her future. Paperback, 2nd printing, 1997. $7.50 (plus shipping and handling).

Waiting for Her Isaac

Sixteen year-old Beth Grant is quite happy with her life and has no desire for any changes. But God has many lessons in store before she is ready for courtship. The story of Beth's spiritual journey toward godly womanhood is told along with the story of her courtship. 1997. $7.50 (plus shipping and handling).

The Farm Mystery Series

Join Jason and Andy as they try to solve the mysterious happenings on the Nelson family's farm. These are books that the whole family will enjoy. In fact, many have used them as read-aloud-to-the-family books. Parents can be assured that there are no murders or other objectionable elements in these books. The boys learn lessons in obedience and responsibility while having lots of fun. There are no worldly situations or language, and no boy-girl relationships. Just happy and wholesome Christian family life, with lots of everyday adventure woven in.

Footprints in the Barn

Who is the man in the green car? What is going on in the hayloft? Is there something wrong with the mailbox? And what's for lunch? The answers to these and many other interesting questions are found in the book Footprints in the Barn. Hardcover. 1996. $12 (plus shipping and handling).

The Mysterious Message

The Great Detective Agency is at it once again, solving mysteries on the Nelson farmstead. Why is there a pile of rocks in the woods? Is someone stealing gas from the mill? How could a railroad disappear? And will Jason and Andy have to eat biscuits without honey? You will have to read this second book in the Farm Mystery Series to find out. Paperback. 1997. $7.50 (plus shipping and handling).

Midnight Sky

What is that sound in the woods? Has someone been stealing Dad's tools? Why is a strange dog barking at midnight? And will the Nelsons be able to adopt Russian children? Midnight Sky provides the answers. Paperback. 1998. $7.50 (plus shipping and handling)

Other Books

Our Homestead Story: The First Years

The humorous account of one family's journey toward a more self-sufficient life-style with the help of God. Read about their experiences with cows, chickens, horses, sheep, gardening and more. Paperback. 1996. $7.50 (plus shipping and handling).

The Orchard Lane Series: In the Spring of the Year

Meet the Hunter family and share in their lives as they move to a new home. The first in our newest series, In the Spring of the Year is written especially for children ages 5-10. Nancy, Caleb, and Emily learn about obedience and self-denial while enjoying the simple pleasures of innocent childhood. Paperback. 1999. $8.00 (plus shipping and handling).

The Delivery

Joe Reynolds is a husband and father striving to live a life pleasing to the Lord Jesus Christ. Having been a Christian only seven years, he has many questions and challenges in his life. How does a man working in the world face temptation? How doe he raise his family in a Christ-honoring way? This book attempts to Biblically address many of the issues that men face daily, in a manner that will not cause the reader to stumble in his walk with the Lord. The book is written for men (and young men) by a man – we ask men to read it first, before reading it aloud to their families. Paperback. 1999. ISBN 1-891907-09-3. $9.00 (plus shipping and handling).

Shipping and Handling Costs

The shipping and handling charge is $2.00 for the first book and 50¢ for each additional book you buy in the same order.

You can save on shipping by getting an order together with your friends or homeschool group. On orders of 10-24 books, shipping is only 50¢ per book. Orders of 25 or more books are shipped FREE. Just have each person write a check for their own total, send in all the checks, and indicate one address for shipping.

To order, please send a check for the total, including shipping (Wisconsin residents, please add 5.5% sales tax on the total, including shipping and handling charges) to:

Castleberry Farms Press • Dept. MM
P.O. Box 337 • Poplar, WI 54864

Please note that prices and shipping charges are subject to change.